A Dark Quill

Tales and Poems

S. B. Lacroix

Published by Tenebrae Publishing.

ISBN-13: 978-0692208229

ISBN-10: 0692208224

Original and modified cover art by Ian Burt and CoverDesignStudio.com

—

Life is a series of events caught in fragments of time in which we find the beauty of the poetic and the reality of the grim.

—

Contents

—

—

"Words have no power to impress the mind without the exquisite horror of their reality." ~ Edgar Allan Poe

Sad To the Bone

Happiness had never really existed. Situations and circumstances masqueraded as such, but genuine happiness had escaped me.

If I had one excuse why it had, I had a thousand, but none of that seemed to matter anymore. Excuses were no longer acceptable. The time had come to face the facts and remove the mask.

Happiness isn't a destination, it's a perception, and mine left me wanting. All the chemical cocktails in the world were not going to change my perception of reality. Numb them or obscure them perhaps, but change them? Not likely.

I'm too this, I'm not enough that—if only I'd stop, if only I'd start. If only I didn't see everything. If only I could close my eyes, and it would all just go away.

Forget who you are and remember who you were, the voice in my head repeated over and over—a chant that became my obsession. Who was I? For that matter, who am I? And what difference would forgetting one to remember the other make?

I wasn't sure, but perhaps it was time to fall into the abyss that had threatened to consume me since my adolescence. Maybe, just maybe, down in that dark hole I feared I'd never find my way out of, was the key I needed to find my way free. And maybe that key that would open a lock that would open a door that I'd walk through, and be able to breathe for once in my life—really breathe, deep and full breaths that would set my soul soaring.

Or maybe I'd fall into that dark abyss and never come back. I'd rot until there was nothing left of me but bones in which the true nature of my sadness would be found.

"She was sad to the bone," the medical examiner would say. "Right to her very bones there was a melancholy so great we've not a name for it."

My skeleton would be erected in a classroom, but not a biology class, in a psychology class.

"See here, we can see this woman was greatly and devastatingly sorrowful," the professor would explain, pointing to various bones the color of tar from the black bile that permeated them.

"Melancholia," he'd announce.

"Depression," he'd state.

"A mood disorder," he'd say in a disapproving tone, shaking his head.

"A broken brain, most certainly insane, with a compulsion to rhyme, tapping her foot and keeping time — a manic depressive, most certainly!"

The class would sit devoid of expression and emotion as they examined the skeleton of a woman whose bones were bad, whose bones were sad, who rotted away in an abyss she so willing let herself fall.

Edgar

The red berries on the bush in the backyard were the only color that bleak morning in November. My eyes sat fixated on their crimson coats, for everything else seemed as dead as I felt.

I sipped my coffee, eyes transfixed, mind blank, body breathing yet dead inside. My skin appeared as grey as the sky that cold morning. My heart broken yet beating, as if to mock my very existence.

There was nothing, there is nothing, and there shall be nothing. Anyone who dared challenge my logic would find themselves cut to shreds by my razor sharp tongue. I had no time for fools, and I would not suffer them. I had suffered enough.

My stomach growled, and I entertained the idea of breakfast, but shuddered at the thought of cooking. Perhaps I could manage to butter a piece of bread and wash it down with a glass of milk. Perhaps I'd just have another cup of coffee.

I pulled myself out of the chair and away from the kitchen table, and shuffled to the counter where the coffee maker sat awaiting my arrival. If only everyone could be as dependable as a coffee maker. If only they'd take their allotted coffee grounds and water and brew the elixir of life. That's what coffee had become since her death. Without it I feared I wouldn't function at all.

I slumped against the kitchen counter whilst exhaling the agony that consumed my heart when I thought of her.

"Vera, my dear Vera, how could you leave me? How could you let death take you away? Why didn't you fight harder? Why didn't death take me as well?" I muttered.

Foolish…it all seemed so foolish. Why did I survive? I had been as sick as she, hadn't I? My fever was higher. I complained more. Vera had been strong, telling me it was just the flu, and that it would pass in time. The only thing that passed in time was Vera. I still felt sick. Only now I was sick in my heart and my mind, as well as my body.

Vera said a lot of things, and a lot of them were untrue. She told me she'd get better. She didn't. She told me she loved only me, but that too was a lie. She denied it, naturally, but I knew. I saw the way she looked at Vincent. I saw the way she longed for his embrace.

"Vera! Can you hear me, Vera? I know you loved him. I know about you and Vincent!"

Nothing — there was never a reply. I often wondered had she really died? Or had she feigned her own demise to be with *him*?

I did not see her body after she had been pronounced dead. Vincent said it was better that way. It would seem madness — nothing but grief-stricken madness — if not for the fact that Vincent was a physician, and he was Vera's physician at that. I couldn't help but wonder if the good doctor had offered Vera a way out of her life with me and in to a life with him. The thought consumed me. It haunted me like a spirit who insistently whispered the name of my beloved Vera.

I thought of the shovel in the garage. I thought of the cemetery and how the cover of night would assist me. I thought about my beautiful Vera, so pure, rotting away like a putrid apple with a worm-riddled core.

So pure — the thought made me laugh. Maybe once, but not after Vincent's filthy hands had run all over her milky-white, flawless skin. The very thought of it made my stomach turn, and I tossed my coffee into the kitchen sink — its milk-white porcelain now stained, just like my Vera.

I felt wretched, my body still weak from the influenza. I made my way to the sofa in the parlor and collapsed.

***

I awoke late that afternoon as the sun was setting. I sat up and found myself feeling much better. I thought about the shovel again. The cover of darkness would be waiting by the time I arrived at the cemetery. I hurried upstairs to dress, and I was off with the shovel in the trunk of my car.

It was dark when I arrived at the cemetery, just as I knew it would be. I parked the car, grabbed the flashlight out of the glove box, and retrieved the shovel from the trunk. I headed towards Vera's grave. At last I'd have my answer. At last I'd have my proof.

The ground was hard, but frost had not yet set in. I began digging. I smirked, feeling invincible. Even if the frost had set in, it would not stop me from unearthing the truth. I smirked again at the play on words my thoughts created, twirling and dancing in my head.

The shovel hit the top of Vera's casket. I felt a rush of excitement. As giddy as a school boy with a crush, I carefully removed the dirt that covered the coffin. What if my beloved Vera was in there? What if she had not betrayed me with Vincent?

I pried open the casket. I fumbled for the flashlight. My heart was pounding in my chest, mocking my existence once more.

There she laid, my beautiful Vera. She did not look like a rotting apple with a worm-riddled core. She looked like a sleeping angel, so pure, so precious. How could I have ever doubted her?

"Oh Vera, will you ever forgive me for doubting you?"

"Edgar," said a voice from above.

I turned, flashlight in hand, and looked upward. I could not believe my eyes. It simply could not be.

"Vincent! What are you doing here?"

———
- 5 -

"Tying up loose ends, of course," Vincent said and hit me in the head with my own shovel. I fell upon my beloved Vera as my head swam and throbbed.

Vincent grabbed hold of my legs and lifted them into the casket. There I lay on top of Vera, face to face. I could smell her death, and the foreboding of mine.

"I had a burning desire for Vera," Vincent began, "but she wouldn't have me. One night I drank too much and forced myself on her. She said she was going to tell you and ruin me. I couldn't allow that to happen."

I felt rage roar deep within, but my head still swam. I wanted to get up, grab the shovel, and beat Vincent to death. I wanted to kick his insides around the graveyard. I wanted to crack open his skull and piss on his brain.

Despite my swimming head, I tried to rise, but Vincent struck me again with the shovel, this time to my upper back. I fell again on top of Vera.

"So, when Vera fell ill," Vincent continued, "I paid her a visit while you were out, and I smothered her with your pillow. Did you hear me, Edgar? I killed her with *your* pillow, and you thought she had succumbed to influenza."

As Vincent laughed, anger consumed me. I wanted him dead. I tried to rise once more to seize Vincent, and end his guffaw along with his life.

Vincent yet again struck me with the shovel. The blow to my head sounded like a crack of thunder.

I thought of Vera. I thought of the red berries on the bush in the backyard with their crimson coats. I thought of the blood trickling down the side of my face staining Vera's ivory laced coffin pillow. I thought of the kitchen sink, stained with coffee and how nothing was pure. I thought how I would become like Vera, with a worm-riddled core.

And then, I thought no more.

In Your Head

I hated the noise and smell of the place, but he made it worth putting up with. I don't know what turned me on more, watching him fight another man and win, or watching him take a beating and give it back in spades. I wasn't a kickboxing fan, not at all. I found the sport barbaric and disgusting, but that was before Ethan Halorand walked into my life.

There was something about Ethan that made it nearly impossible for me to take my eyes off him, but I wasn't sure what it was.

Ethan was of average height and intelligence. He kept himself in shape, but wasn't extremely muscular. He wore his dark hair quite short, and was fairly attractive. There wasn't anything remarkable about Ethan really, except maybe his soul. There was something inside that man that burned hot—a fiery passion, or a raging anger. I had glimpsed it through his hazel eyes on more than one occasion. Each time I had my pulse quickened.

Ethan had scars, inside and out. I knew this because I knew Ethan, but Ethan didn't know me, not really. Sometimes I wished he did, but that wasn't possible, and there were plenty of reasons why.

Women of my social standing did not date men of Ethan's. As snobbish as that seemed, it was fact. Ethan worked the docks, loading and unloading cargo. I was a physician, a psychiatrist to be more specific. I was also married.

My husband Jeff was a banker with a penchant for scotch and young women. Any woman over the age of twenty-five was too old for Jeff. I was twenty-five plus twenty.

Ethan was thirty-three and a patient of mine, which made him off limits. It was unethical for me as a physician to become sexually involved with a patient, and as a psychiatrist, it was a forever kind of unethical. The loss of one's license to practice was the cost of such behavior. Of all the reasons I could never see Ethan socially, the relationship I had with him was the most restrictive of them all.

It was part of my job to observe Ethan, and I did it well. I even took my work home, so to speak. I would attend Ethan's kickboxing matches to watch him, to observe him. I wore a wig and dark glasses so I could sit close enough to see him sweat. I enjoyed watching him bleed. I enjoyed watching him make another man bleed. I enjoyed watching him release that inner fire, that inner anger he couldn't seem to in my office.

Ethan was compact and powerful, quick and accurate. He struck his opponent with precision and with intent. The sounds of flesh hitting flesh aroused me. Amongst the cheering and shouting of the cramped and over heated arena, I'd often daydream of the sexual positions in which Ethan's skin would hit mine. I indulged myself with thoughts of his stamina, of his fiery passion, of his brute force, taking me again and again. How I managed a thought of my own in that noisy, human-packed place amazed me. Either I was really good at focusing on my thoughts, or I was really hot for Ethan. I suspected it was a bit of both.

I never felt guilty about my daydreams, not where Jeff was concerned anyway. He was forever out with his pals, boozing and bedding college girls. If my conscience bothered me anywhere it was with my profession. I was tiptoeing around the rules, and I knew it was wrong. I had worked too hard to get where I was to blow it all on a lusty crush I had on a guy who worked at the docks, and who seemed to enjoy beating the crap out of other men.

My desire for Ethan had become a problem for me, but I refused to confide in any of my colleagues about it. I didn't want help getting over my feelings. I wanted them. I needed them. My life with Jeff was dull and unfulfilling. Ethan made me feel young, alive, and sexy. I knew I couldn't allow my desire for Ethan to get the best of me, even though at times it threatened to.

In session, Ethan had yet to talk about his intimate relationships. One session he told me about a guy on the docks who had pissed him off. I entertained the thought he might be gay, and his inability to come out was the catalyst for his anger. Part of me hoped he was gay. I reasoned if he were gay then the fact I was his doctor wouldn't matter, neither would the fact I was married, or our difference in age or social status — all of it would be irrelevant. He would find no interest in my large breasts, my curvaceous figure, or any of my feminine attributes. I would lack the equipment he desired, and that would be the end of it. There would be no hope despite all the obstacles, and maybe I could let go of the idea of Ethan in my bed.

One rainy afternoon Ethan had been at my office. He was having a particularly hard time talking about what he was feeling. I sat twirling my shoulder-length blonde hair around my finger, fantasizing about straddling him while he sat in the chair, my bare breasts in his face. He looked at me, *really* looked at me. I stopped twirling. I held my breath and thought, this was it — this was the moment he would confess he was gay and explain why he couldn't tell anyone. All that anger would finally have its genesis revealed.

"The way you twirl your hair reminds me of an ex-girlfriend," Ethan began. "She was blonde with big breasts, and sexy, like you. It's too bad she was such a bitch. I really enjoyed her…if you know what I mean."

I took a deep breath, remained silent, and vowed never to twirl my hair again while Ethan was in my office. The impossible had been confirmed as possible. He wasn't gay. I had the right equipment, and he found me desirable. The other obstacles could be overcome, even if they shouldn't be, and that scared me.

The roar of the arena rose loud enough to bring me out of my head and aware of my surroundings. Ethan had won the match, but he looked a bit worse for wear. He was due in my office the following afternoon. He had recently started coming to see me weekly instead of twice a month. He had explained he was having a hard time controlling his impulses, but had yet to confide in me what those impulses were.

I made my way through the crowd and out of the arena to the parking lot. It was pouring, and I was soaking wet by the time I got into the car. I looked in the rearview mirror to check my mascara. My chestnut eyes peered back at me with accusation. What I wanted had the power to ruin me, yet somehow that made me want it all the more.

***

The next day I had to force myself to stay focused on my patients. I found myself doodling on my note pad as they talked. It seemed there was a theme amongst them, and that theme was sex — a theme my mind didn't need on the day Ethan was coming in.

First there was the chronically depressed Mrs. Wallace, who droned on about her teenage son and how his hyper-sexuality was an embarrassment to the entire family.

"…and if I catch him masturbating again in the family room while watching that filthy pornography, I don't know what I'll do. Just because it's in the middle of the night, and he thinks we're all asleep, doesn't mean it's alright. It's the family room, for heaven's sake."

The more she went on about the sex drive of her seventeen-year-old son, the more I thought of Ethan, and wondered what he was like at seventeen.

Next there was Mr. Jenkins, a man in his early sixties who had bipolar disorder. He'd been married since his mid-twenties and had homosexual tendencies he had suppressed all his life. The poor man wasn't just in the closet; he was locked in it since he refused to come clean with his wife. He'd usually go on about the young men he'd meet at the gym, their hard bodies, and how he wanted to have sex with them, but apparently Mr. Jenkins had stepped over the line of lust and into the action.

"I couldn't believe it. There I was in the locker room with this young, hot guy and he's letting me….umm….you know, put his….you know, in my mouth…and…" Mr. Jenkins's voice trailed off as he looked at the floor.

"You seem embarrassed to tell me what happened," I said.

"Well, kind of. I don't want to offend you, Dr. Harper."

"I appreciate that, Jay. I gather you had oral sex with a young man in the locker room?"

"Did I ever. I was on my knees and…"

Any embarrassment Jay Jenkins had abruptly left as he went on about his encounter — the size of the young man's penis, and how excited it made him to finally be acting on his repressed sexual desires. With each descriptive detail he gave I thought of Ethan, imagining he was the young man in the locker room, and I was the one on my knees.

"Were you manic when this happened, Jay?" I interrupted.

"Ah…well, I must have been. I don't think I would have had the guts to do it otherwise."

"I see, maybe we should get another blood level and see if an increase in your medication is necessary."

"You're the doctor, whatever you think is best, but can I finish telling you about it?"

"I don't need to hear the—"

"And then I asked him if I could…" he interrupted, his voice fading in my mind.

Jay Jenkins wasn't going to allow me to deny him the pleasure of telling the entire story of his first homosexual experience, even if he risked offending me. I let him have at it, doodling on my note pad, thinking about Ethan.

My next patient was Ms. Lexton, a young woman in her early twenties, also bipolar, who complained about her inability to control her desire to have sex with random men. She wanted me to give her a new medication. What she really wanted me to do was to chemically abort the desire to bed every desirable man she came across.

"Just give me something to make it stop. Don't you have a pill that will make me not want to have sex or something?"

I shook my head.

"Why the hell do I even bother to come here?"

"Annie, you know—"

She flipped me the middle finger, got up, and stormed out of the office, mumbling something about getting high. She was far less interested in managing her illness than she was in getting some fix, any fix that would stop what she was feeling.

I understood her plight, but medication didn't work that way. If there were such a pill, I might have taken it to end my desire for Ethan.

I looked at the clock across the room and felt excitement flutter in my chest. It was Ethan time. I grabbed the mirror I kept in my desk drawer and checked my makeup. I reapplied my lipstick and fluffed my hair. I repositioned my breasts in my bra, stood up, and straightened my skirt. I then walked to the waiting room.

"Ethan, would you come in, please?" I asked.

He looked up at me and smiled.

I turned and walked back to my office as he followed me down the hall. I could feel myself allowing my hips swaying more than usual as I walked. I had on a new pair of heels that were higher than I normally wore, so I took my time with each step. The last thing I wanted to do was fall.

"I love it when women wear sexy shoes," Ethan said just as I went to take my seat.

I missed my chair, and my ass hit the floor.

"Are you alright? Let me help you up."

Ethan put his hands under my arms and pulled me to my feet. My face flushed, and I felt foolish. I didn't want to look him in the eye, but I did. He wasn't looking at my face, however; he was looking at my breasts.

My first instinct was to pull away, but I fought it. I stood there my heart pounding, half with excitement, half with embarrassment. I kept looking him in the eye. He looked up and met my gaze.

"Sorry, I shouldn't have, but you are doubly blessed," he said and smiled.

"Thank you for helping me up, Ethan, please have a seat."

He sat in the chair opposite me as he usually did, but something was different. It seemed as if the invisible barrier I tried so hard to keep between us was gone. It appeared I wasn't the only one who noticed.

"Are you married, Helen?" Ethan asked.

"Dr. Harper, please," I replied.

"Sorry, I shouldn't have asked."

"No, that's fine. Yes, I'm married."

"But not happily?"

"That really isn't your business, Ethan."

"Mr. Halorand, please," said Ethan.

The game had begun. It was a game of seeing who'd cross the line and dare to stay there. Crossing it was easy, it was the staying there that would prove challenging.

"Fine, Mr. Halorand, would you like to talk about the impulses you are finding it harder to control?"

"Well you see, Dr. Harper, the harder it gets, the more difficult the impulse is to control."

I watched his face without blinking before forming my reply. Was he playing silly word games with me, or was I reading sexual innuendos into his words? For the first time in the nine months I had been treating Ethan for his anger issues and depression, I thought maybe my lust for him was getting in the way of my ability to treat him.

"I'm not sure I understand what you mean. What impulse are you referring to?" I asked without making any facial expression.

"Sexual impulse, Dr. Harper, I can't control a sexual impulse I'm having."

"Can you be more specific?"

"Are you sure you want me to?"

Again I paused to watch his face before forming a reply. I couldn't read anything from his expression.

"Yes," I answered.

"Alright, just remember you said yes."

Ethan stood up and walked towards me.

"Mr. Halorand, what are you doing?"

"Being more specific," Ethan replied as he bent over, reached for my breasts, and with a breast in each hand, his lips met mine.

In my mind I could see myself falling into him, allowing him to do whatever he wanted right there in my office. I imagined him leading me over to my desk, pulling up my skirt, and taking me from behind.

I pushed my chair back as I stood up. I did my best to appear as if I were appalled by his actions.

"Mr. Halorand, I think it best I refer you to another psychiatrist."

"You mean you already forgot?"

"Forgot what?" I asked feeling slightly confused.

"That you said yes."

I ran my hands through my hair, my mind and heart racing.

Goddamn little shit. Who the hell does he think he is?

I wanted to slap him across the face. I wanted to make him bleed. I wanted his sweat all over my body.

"You're not here to play games, Mr. Halorand. I will have my secretary call you with a referral. I would like you to leave my office. Now, please."

I walked over to the door and opened it.

Ethan sat down in defiance.

"Mr. Halorand, I would like you to—"

"Sweat all over you, after you make me bleed? Do you want to hurt me, Dr. Harper?"

I stood dumbfounded. I shut the office door and sat down in my chair. The look on my face said what I couldn't. He knew, but how?

"I know what you're thinking. You know, ESP?" Ethan said as if he were answering my questioning thought.

I was surprised he thought I'd buy that ESP boloney. He must have found out some how. Some one must have told him. Maybe he saw me at one of his kickboxing matches.

His face lit up. "You go to my matches? You like kickboxing?"

I sat expressionless. I didn't believe Ethan's claim, but I thought about Jeff liquored up on scotch, overweight and balding, prowling for young women to defile...just in case.

"I asked you about kickboxing, and if you go to my matches, and you're thinking about Jeff?"

"Mr. Halorand, I'm not sure what is happening here, but it is clear you should seek treatment from another psychiatrist."

"I don't get it. You're supposed to help me, but now because I know things I shouldn't, you tell me to get another shrink?"

"That's not it at all."

"No? Then what is it? Please, Dr. Harper, tell me."

I stood up and walked over to my desk. He must have seen me at one of his matches, and he could have easily found out Jeff's name. It was a coincidence, or a lucky guess. He couldn't know my thoughts. I didn't believe in extrasensory perception, or telepathy, or any of that New Age bullshit.

"I have never seen you at one of my matches, and why don't you believe in ESP or telepathy? It's not bullshit."

I turned and looked at him, horrified.

What on earth was this madness? I suddenly realized how my psychotic patients must have felt when I told them what they believed to be real, actually wasn't. *It's in your head.* How many times had I had to say that to them? How many times had I looked upon their faces, every one of them washed with confusion, and tried to explain that what they believed to be factual, wasn't reality, but a figment of their imagination? How many times had I caused another person to feel as unsure of what was real as I did at this moment?

"Who's to say what's real and what isn't?" Ethan mused aloud.

He looked at me and smirked.

I looked back at him, still horrified.

Were my thoughts really not my own? Either Ethan was reading my mind, or I was losing my grip on reality. My training automatically steered me towards the latter.

I sat down, shaking. I took a deep breath, tried to calm myself, and regain my composer, all without thinking anything I didn't want Ethan to know.

"For nine months I've sat in this chair," Ethan began, "telling you my thoughts while listening to yours. I know you want me, and all the ways in which you'd like to have me. I thought it was time you knew I want you too.

You know, when you thought I might be gay, that really pissed me off. You really had the wrong end of the stick on that one. That's why I made a point to tell you about my ex-girlfriend in our next session."

"Whatever is going on here is not…right. It's not healthy for you, and I could get in trouble—ah…I mean it's not…um…" I couldn't speak properly.

"I would never tell anyone, Helen. I don't want people to know I hear thoughts, or read minds, or whatever it is I do. I don't want people to think I'm a freak, and I wouldn't want you to get into trouble."

Thoughts about Ethan's abilities started creeping into my mind like insects I couldn't control. He looked at me as if he could read my every thought as easily as he could read a book. If only I were fluent in another language—one Ethan didn't know—my thoughts would be out of his reach.

"Yeah, I only speak English too," Ethan said and winked at me.

I wanted to slap him upside the head, the cocky little bastard. Another thought began forming in my mind, one I didn't want Ethan to know. I started thinking about the lyrics to a Rolling Stones song.

"Ethan, I have to go to the restroom. I'll be back in a moment. Will you wait here for me, please?"

"Yeah, sure," Ethan replied and began humming the tune to *Gimme Shelter*, the song I had been silently singing.

"I like that song too," he said, as if we were having a normal conversation.

I stood up, hurried out of the office, down the hall, and into the restroom. I locked the door and leaned against the wall to gather myself. I needed to know if he could hear my thoughts when I wasn't near him. Just how far away would I need to be in order to be safe from his invasion of my mind? I figured I'd have to test it.

I thought about my cat, Isis. I pictured her in my mind. I thought about the black sheen of her fur, her pretty golden-yellow eyes, and how she rubbed up against my leg. I thought about my cat as hard as I could, and then I thought about Ethan asking me about my cat.

I left the restroom. As I walked down the hall I started silently repeating part of a poem by Emily Dickinson so I wouldn't think of my cat or her name. I kept repeating the same two lines of the poem as I turned the doorknob on the office door, but once I opened the door, I stopped.

I sat down in my chair and refuse to allow my previous thoughts into my head. I remained silent. I looked at Ethan waiting for him to speak. I imagined the sound of a clock ticking in my head and nothing else.

Ethan stared at me with an odd look on his face. He tilted his head to the right as if he were listening to something, or trying to process information.

"Tick-tock, tick-tock, tick-tock," Ethan muttered. "What's up with that?"

"Well, Ethan, time is almost up. Why don't we end the session for today, and we'll meet next week, same time."

Ethan sighed.

"In the meantime, I'll do some research and try to find out if there is some explanation for what's happening, other than extrasensory perception. We'll have to discuss what has been unearthed here today in detail and make a decision from there." I bluffed.

"Some other explanation for what's happening?" Ethan said and smiled. "We can go that route if you want, I guess, but no telling anyone else about this. You keep my secrets, I keep yours, deal?"

"Of course, it's a bond that will bring us closer," I lied.

Ethan looked at me, his eyes narrowing, as if he questioned my truthfulness, but said nothing. He stood up, walked towards me, and kissed me on the cheek.

For a moment I felt guilty for deceiving him, but forced myself to think about my lust for him instead. The last thing I wanted him sensing was my guilt. It seemed impossible to have a feeling without a thought that preceded it.

Ethan left as if it was any other session. It was anything but. I was filled with a mixture of arousal and dread.

My lies had bought me some time, but he knew my deepest secret now. I might as well have verbally told him all the things I thought about while he sat across from me in session those nine months. They were inappropriate, to say the least. If he ever told someone, if he filed a complaint, it could be the end of my career.

My little experiment on how far away I needed to be for Ethan not to be able to invade my mind gave me some comfort. He didn't mention my cat or her name, and he didn't mention the poem I repeated as I opened the door. Also, it seemed he was unaware I went to his kickboxing matches until I thought about it in the office with him present. It appeared he could only hear my thoughts if I was in very close proximity to him. I hoped I was right.

What to do about the matter was what I'd spend my week figuring out. It didn't matter if it was extrasensory perception or something else, all that mattered is he knew my sexual thoughts about him. All those months of sessions, and I now understood why he'd look away, smile out of the blue, or just sit quietly as if he were listening to something far away.

I shuddered at the thought of him knowing the things I thought while at his kickboxing matches. Those fantasies were laced with violence. Even if I didn't lose my license—after all I never acted on any of my thoughts—I should have referred him to another psychiatrist the moment I realized my desire for him. Clearly it was inhibiting my ability to treat him. That's what they'd say, and they'd be right.

What could be proven really didn't matter, not at this point. I crossed a line, even if it was only mentally. No one was ever supposed to know, especially not Ethan Halorand.

***

The week passed, and I had mixed feelings about the speed in which it did. Part of me wanted the week to go by slowly so I could have more time to think and plan. Another part of me wanted it to go by quickly so I could see Ethan again. No matter what I wanted, the time had passed, and there sat Ethan Halorand in my office once again. I only hoped I could keep myself from thinking things I didn't want him to know.

"How are you today, Ethan?" I asked.

"I'm fine, Helen. How are you?"

He was using my first name again, but after our last session, what did I expect?

"Listen, Ethan, I've done some research. It could be extrasensory perception. It could also be a very rare and serious mental illness," I lied.

Ethan looked concerned and leaned forward.

"Like what?" he asked.

"Well, it's quite rare and not well understood. I think it might be best if you saw a specialist."

"No," Ethan said shaking his head. "You treat me. I'm not going anywhere else."

I had expected him to respond that way.

"You knew I'd say no?" Ethan demanded.

"Hearing my thoughts again?"

"I heard you think you expected I'd respond that way."

"Well, that's because I did."

"So what do we do?" he asked.

"Well, I will give you a medication to try, and we'll see how it works for you."

"And what do we do about the other thing?"

"What other thing?" I asked feigning ignorance.

"The sexual tension between us, Helen, you know exactly what I'm talking about."

"Well, I think we should try to get you well before we consider that, don't you?"

"Assuming I'm sick and not simply telepathic, you mean?"

"Yes, of course."

"Lying bitch," Ethan said and clenched his jaw.

"Ethan, I—"

"What were you going to give me," Ethan interrupted, "some medication that would leave me incoherent and drooling? There is no mental illness that is causing me to hear your thoughts. I am telepathic. I always have been. I just wanted to see if you'd be honest with me. I thought we had an understanding? You know a bond that would bring us closer? Wasn't that your line?"

I didn't know how to respond. I swallowed hard and studied his face.

"I trusted you. I thought you cared about me. I care deeply for you, Helen."

"I do care about you, Ethan. That is why I suggested you see another—"

"Oh really," Ethan interrupted, "is that why you want to make me bleed? Let's be honest, shall we?"

"I'm trying to be."

"Stop lying, Helen."

"Ethan, I'm doing my best to be honest with you. Clearly you don't appreciate the enormity of the situation."

"I what—just how stupid do you think I am?"

I tried not to think anything. I imagined my mind as a blank slate.

"You're right, I must be stupid. I thought we had something here, Helen. I thought we'd have some fun, you know? And then maybe we'd…I don't know, get serious or something.

You don't love your husband. I know you don't. No woman who loves her husband thinks what you think about him."

Well, he's right about Jeff….shit…my mind is a blank slate…

"I knew it. I knew you didn't love him, and stop with the stupid blank slate shit."

Ethan was clearly agitated. He had been on the edge of his seat the whole time, but now he stood up and began pacing. He walked behind my chair, and it made me nervous. I turned around and watched him remove a roll of duct tape from the pocket of his jacket.

"Ethan, what are you doing?" I asked, my voice giving my fear way.

"Giving you what you want, Helen," Ethan responded. His voice was flat, lacking any emotion, even anger.

I listened to the sound of the duct tape being pulled from the roll, my body frozen with fear. The thought of screaming or running out of the office barely entered my mind when Ethan grabbed me and quickly put duct tape over my mouth. He seemed to know my thoughts before I completed them. He seemed all powerful.

Ethan then bound my hands behind me at the wrists. I tried to fight him, but he slapped me hard in the face, causing me to sway, and lose my bearings. He then bound my ankles.

The left side of my face throbbed as I recalled my observations of Ethan Halorand and how accurate they had been. He was compact and powerful, quick and accurate. He struck his opponent with precision and with intent.

I could feel fear pulsing through my veins, invading every cell in my body, and yet at the same time, I found myself sexually aroused. There was a part of me that relished this arousal, and a part of me that was disgusted by it. It was Ethan's anger that excited me. It was Ethan's power over me that made me go wobbly in the knees despite the seriousness of the situation.

Ethan put his hands under my arms and helped me over to my desk. He was sweating, and I could smell it.

He cleared my desk with one swipe of his arm. He pushed my head down onto the desk. My feet remained on the floor, but from the waist up my body lay on the desk. I was bent over my desk just as I had imagined all those times, minus the duct tape. When bondage entered my fantasies, it was not I who was bound.

Ethan put his cheek against the desk and looked at me. The anger had faded from his eyes, and I saw something softer envelope them.

"Now Helen," he began, "I can either leave you here like this, or I can give you what you want, but you have to admit you want it. Remember, I can hear what you think."

I felt helpless both physically and mentally. He already knew what I wanted. There was no point in trying to lie. I realized there was no point in speaking either. I could admit what I wanted with my thoughts, and maybe if I thought about it the way I wanted it, that's what he'd give me.

I thought about Ethan removing the duct tape and kissing me passionately. I thought about him pulling up my skirt, ripping off my panties, and taking me from behind. I thought about his passion. I thought about his power. I thought about his sweat on my skin.

Ethan smiled. He removed his jacket and shirt. He removed the duct tape from my ankles and my wrists. He removed it from my mouth last, which hurt the most.

He kissed me, as if to offer an apology for the pain removing the tape had caused. He then removed my blouse and my bra. He hiked up my skirt and ripped off my panties. He bent me over my desk, and he entered me.

I felt my body being thrust against the desk. I felt Ethan's sweat drip onto my back, but it was nothing like my fantasies. Ethan put on a great show when kickboxing, but when it came to getting down to business, he lacked the passion I imagined him to have. The act was mechanical and over rather quickly. I found myself disgusted and utterly disappointed. I couldn't even look at him.

"Not as good as you imagined, Helen?" Ethan said.

I heard the zip of his fly and the buckling of his belt.

"That's a shame. Maybe under different circumstances I can live up to your expectations. I'd be happy to work at it." His voice was heavy with sarcasm.

I was going to say it, but then I thought, why bother?

Jeff has done me better than that, Ethan. But then again, he screws young women on a regular basis, so he gets lots of practice.

"You bitch," he said. His tone suggested my thought had emotionally wounded him.

"There's a reason your husband is out screwing young women, Helen. If you could see your ass from this view, you'd know what I mean."

And his dick is bigger too.

WHAM. Pain radiated through my head. Ethan had palmed the back of my head like a basketball and slam dunked it against my desk. I focused on the pain as I pulled myself across the top of the desk. Ethan was laughing. I hoped his amusement of the situation would keep his mind preoccupied. I opened the top middle drawer and fumbled around its contents until my fingers felt the shape of it.

"What are you doooing, Helleeen?" Ethan sang as he grabbed my ankles, pulling me towards him, my feet again touching the floor.

I stood up, turned quickly, and plunged the letter opener into Ethan's stomach.

He gasped and looked at me, shock replacing the smug look I imagined he possessed when he had sung my name.

He put his hands over mine, attempting to remove the letter opener. He succeeded in pulling it back a few fractions of an inch before I plunged it deeper.

Ethan stood with his mouth hanging open, blood oozing from the wound in his abdomen. I watched as the crimson stream of his blood tainted the exquisite pattern of my oriental rug when I realized, I had made Ethan Halorand bleed.

I had fantasized about making him bleed, but never did I envision a grave wound, merely playful ones. Ethan's sweating and bleeding proved to be like the sex—bitterly disappointing.

I stepped away from him and watched as he fell to his knees, and then to his side. He groaned in pain. Concerned he might yell for help, I picked my blouse up off the floor, and stuffed as much of it as I could into his mouth. His hazel eyes, swimming with betrayal, looked into mine, and I felt sorry it had come to this. I sat down on the floor and leaned close to him.

"I'm sorry, but you left me no choice," I whispered in his ear. I kissed his cheek and licked my lips. I could taste the salt of his sweat. He tasted good. I ran my hands over his biceps as he clutched the letter opener in his stomach. He felt good.

What a waste. If only you had kept your mouth shut, Ethan, and never told me you could hear my thoughts. I wonder…can you hear them now?

Ethan was beginning to lose consciousness. It appeared he wasn't able to process a thought, let alone hear mine.

I picked up my bra and put it on. I took my blouse out of his mouth, put it on, and tore it. I then tore my skirt. I messed up my hair and smudged my makeup. I picked up the roll of duct tape and bound my ankles. I picked up some of the tape he had removed from me and wrapped it around one of my wrists, hoping to give the appearance I had managed to free my hands from being bound.

Ethan had grown quiet and still. I checked to see if he was breathing. He wasn't. I felt for a pulse—dead.

I took a deep breath and screamed. It was only a matter of seconds before the secretary and another doctor burst through the door of my office, and found me in tears on the floor, and Ethan in a pool of his own blood.

**

I was unaware Ethan had a criminal record for violence. (He had lied when I questioned him if he had ever been arrested due to an impulse caused by his anger.) His record consisted of minor assault charges, mostly from bar fights, but having such a history worked in my favor.

I claimed Ethan had come on to me in the session prior to our last, and I had suggested he see another psychiatrist for treatment. I stated that he had said and done things that were inappropriate, which caused me to believe he had developed sexual, even romantic, feelings for me. I explained we had agreed to discuss the move in our next session, however; when I brought it up the following week, Ethan became agitated, bound me with duct tape, and sexually assaulted me.

I continued my explanation that after the assault, I retrieved the letter opener for protection and a struggle ensued. I explained that I believed the struggle was Ethan trying to disarm me of the letter opener, but I was mistaken as it was with his hands over mine that he plunged the letter opener into his own abdomen. I stated that I tried to pull it out, when he resisted, and thrust it in deeper.

I theorized he most likely entertained fantasies that I too found him sexually attractive, and that I had romantic feelings for him as well. When I suggested he seek treatment elsewhere, he took this as my rejection of him and of his feelings for me. This led him to become extremely agitated and in this state, he sexually assaulted me, satisfying both his sexual urges and anger impulse.

As his psychiatrist, I stated I believed his suicide was a shamed based impulse. It was my assessment that he both admired and respected me, and perhaps even thought he loved me. Given this, he simply could not live with what he had done, hence his suicide. The letter opener had been conveniently within his reach, lending ease to his impulse to end his shame for assaulting me, and ultimately his life.

A full investigation of the case was launched. An autopsy of Ethan's body was preformed, and it concluded loss of blood caused from a puncture wound to his abdomen with a sharp object had caused his death.

I was subjected to a full physical examination where Ethan's semen was found inside me, and the bruise to my face where he had struck me was photographed.

After the investigation and my deposition, it was concluded that I had been sexually assaulted by my patient Ethan Halorand, and his death was ruled a suicide.

***

I took time off from work after the incident. Jeff seemed sympathetic towards me. He stopped boozing and bedding young women for nearly a month before deciding I needed time to be alone with my thoughts.

I returned seeing patients, but found it nearly impossible to treat young, attractive men. I was never sure if one of them would end up in my head, like Ethan had. The thought unnerved me.

The medical director suggested since I was having difficulty seeing young, male patients, (which he assumed stemmed from the sexual assault I claimed I had been a victim of) then perhaps I should teach instead. I decided it was an excellent idea, and I began teaching at a local college.

I've been teaching for about three months now. There is a student of mine who is fairly attractive and of average intelligence. He struggles with the work I assign in class. I often stay late to help him with his homework. His name is Max Merone.

There is something about Max that makes it nearly impossible for me to take my eyes off him, but I'm not sure what it is.

The Crows

The crows flew overhead, cawing. They perched on tree tops and squawked messages I was not able to decipher. Perhaps their caws were a calling, but to whom? To other crows, more messengers of doom?

The day darkened as the sky threatened. The crows remained on their tree-top perch seemingly without care. They cawed and squawked away the day. Time seemed to matter little to them.

A clap of thunder followed a bolt of lightening. The crows took flight, their black wings flapping in the opposite direction of the ominous clouds that were rolling in.

I sat pondering, were they messengers of impending change? Or were they simply silly birds looking for a place to perch and squawk, leaving when spooked by thunder?

Perhaps it was a bit of both.

The Spiral of Blood

Charlene thought she was special. She thought a powerful deity watched over her. She thought this deity, venerated by many, favored her because she was gifted, and because she was chosen.

Whenever someone offended her, she would call to her deity and ask for vengeance. Nothing pleased her more than watching others suffer for slighting her, even if these slights existed only in her mind.

Most people who came to know Charlene realized she was vain, yet only those who got to know her well knew she was also thin-skinned. Charlene liked people to think she was fearless, but in truth she was riddled with fear. She had watched her mother die a slow, painful death from cancer and feared she might meet a similar fate.

Friends came and went in Charlene's life. Even childhood friends eventually faded away. Charlene would take offense to something a friend said or did and create conflict, especially where there was none. Even her closest friends, those who truly cared for her, eventually left because of her need to engage in battles of some kind. If she wasn't fighting with others, she was fighting with herself.

She was a short woman with a stocky build. She held her mouth in such a way that it appeared as if she were always pouting. She had an upturned nose which gave a physical bearing to the snobbish attitude she most always had.

One morning while out for a walk in an attempt to work off the fat that stubbornly clung to her waist and thighs, she passed a storefront window. A shiny object caught her eye, and she entered the store.

"Welcome to Heller's Antiques," the saleswoman greeted her. "May I help you?"

The woman had a thick accent Charlene didn't recognize. She had black hair and piercing dark eyes. The numerous metal bracelets she wore made a tinkling sound when she moved her arms.

She dresses like a Gypsy, Charlene thought, holding back a laugh. *Does she think every day is Halloween?*

"I saw something in the window that caught my eye," Charlene replied and walked over to where she had seen the object.

"Allow me to assist you, please. We prefer customers do not reach into the window display," the woman said.

Charlene ignored her and reached into the display. She grabbed the shiny object that had caught her eye. It was a necklace made of white metal with a large circular pendant. Etched into the pendant was a design in form of a spiral that had been enameled in red. Charlene was taken with the piece. She felt as if it spoke to her, as if it was pulling her towards it.

"Is this sterling silver or silver plated?" Charlene asked.

"Please, allow me," the saleswoman replied extending her hand. Charlene placed the necklace in the woman's hand.

"It is neither," the woman answered, without looking at the piece. She then walked over to the sales counter, the necklace still in her hand.

"Well if it's not sterling or even silver plated, I'm not paying much for it," Charlene said in her usual snooty tone.

"You wish to purchase it?" the woman asked.

"Yes, I do. I'll give you ten dollars for it. It's probably some cheap metal that will turn my skin green."

"I'm sorry," the saleswoman began, "but this piece is priced at five hundred dollars."

"What? Charlene asked. "It must be white gold then?"

"No, it is neither silver nor gold."

"Well it can't be platinum at that price, can it?"

"No, it is not."

"Then why the hell is it so much money?"

"Five hundred dollars is the price," the woman responded, ignoring Charlene's question.

"Look lady, I'll give you ten bucks and that's it. It's made of crap metal and is most likely some piece of junk."

"Then why do you desire it if you believe it is worthless?"

"I told you, it caught my eye in the window."

The saleswoman smiled and placed the necklace on the glass counter in front of her.

"It catches many an eye, but few are destined to own it," she said.

"Why is that?" Charlene asked. Her curiosity now piqued.

The saleswoman pulled a book from the shelf behind her. It was a small book, and looked old and worn. She placed it on the counter next to the necklace.

"This explains all," she said, gesturing towards the book.

Charlene picked up the book and opened it. It was written in a language she didn't recognize.

"What language is this?"

"If you do not know, you are not destined to own the Spiral of Blood."

Charlene looked up at the woman, her eyes widening, "The Spiral of Blood?"

"Yes," the saleswoman replied and took the book out of Charlene's hand. "You have heard of it?"

"Of course," Charlene lied. "I just didn't realize what it was when I picked it up. How silly of me. Five hundred dollars you said? You take credit cards, right?"

"I am sorry, no sale," the woman said. "The Spiral of Blood can only be owned by those who are destined to possess it. If you cannot read the sacred book, it is not your destiny."

Charlene became annoyed, and her face grew hot.

"Just because I can't read that book doesn't mean the necklace shouldn't be mine. You said five hundred dollars. You want cash instead? I'll go to the ATM machine across the street and be back in five minutes."

"The necklace is not for sale to you," the woman said. She walked from behind the counter and towards the window display.

Charlene followed her. "If it's so precious that it must be destined to a certain buyer, why isn't it locked up in a glass case?" she asked. "Someone could steal it."

"No one can steal the Spiral of Blood," the woman replied. It is protected by Maehaem."

Charlene gasped and cupped her hand over her mouth. The woman looked at her with narrowed eyes.

"You recognize this name?" the woman asked.

"Yes," Charlene answered truthfully. "Maehaem is my patron Goddess. I am devoted to her. I have a corner in my home dedicated to her veneration. So you see I am destined to own that necklace."

The woman laughed. "You think you are the only one who venerates Maehaem? How foolish you must be."

Anger filled Charlene. *What a stupid bitch,* she thought. *She clearly does not understand the relationship I have with Maehaem.*

"How much do you want for it? I will pay any amount. Name your price."

"It is not the price that matters. If you are not destined to own this necklace, it can be dangerous to possess. Only one who is destined can own the Spiral of Blood pendant."

"But I am destined," Charlene said. "You don't understand who I am. Maehaem has chosen me, and I have a close relationship with her. She has given me special gifts."

"Then you can read the sacred book? Those truly chosen by Maehaem can read the sacred book even if they do not know the language."

Charlene walked back to the counter and picked up the book. She attempted to read as the sales woman watched. Charlene was so focused on trying to read a language she had never seen, she hardly noticed someone had entered the store.

"I didn't realize we had a customer, Adira," said a man's voice. "I thought I'd come see if you wanted lunch."

Charlene looked up from the book and saw an elderly man dressed in trousers, a button up shirt, and sweater. He did not have an accent like the sales woman. Charlene thought he must be the owner, and Adira might be a disgruntled employee who wanted the necklace for herself.

"Are you the owner?" Charlene asked the elderly man.

"Yes, I am," he answered. "My name is Mr. Heller, nice to meet you." He extended his hand to Charlene who did not offer hers in return.

"I'd like to purchase the necklace in your display window, but your sales clerk will not sell it to me despite the fact I am willing to pay the asking price. I suspect she wants it for herself," Charlene said.

Mr. Heller looked at Adira who met his gaze, glanced over at the book in Charlene's hands, met Mr. Heller's eyes once more, and shook her head.

"Does she want the book too? Is that the problem, Adira?" Mr. Heller asked.

"No, the book is my personal possession. It is not for sale. The problem is she cannot read it. She is not destined to own the sacred Spiral of Blood pendant," Adira explained.

"Well now, dear, I understand you have your customs, but if this lady would like to purchase…" Mr. Heller's voice trailed off as Adira glared at him.

"They are not customs. They are sacred laws. She must be destined or the Spiral of Blood cannot be possessed by her," Adira said.

"I suppose you think you are destined to own it?" Charlene asked Adira with a contemptuous sneer.

"Of course I do not think such a thing. You are an ignorant woman. You insult me, and you insult Maehaem."

"Now hold on a minute," Mr. Heller began, "I can't have you speaking to a customer like that. I'll handle this from here, Adira."

Adira glowered at Charlene as she walked past her and into the backroom.

Charlene smirked at the thought of her first victory and looked forward to her second: the purchase of the necklace.

"So how much?" she asked Mr. Heller.

"Make me an offer I cannot refuse. If you make me an offer I can refuse, you will not be allowed to make another, so make your offer well," he replied.

Charlene feared making an offer too low. *What if the old man had been listening in the back room the whole time?* She thought. *What if he heard me say I'd pay any price?*

"How about you just tell me what you want for it and I'll pay it, alright? I have a credit card right here," Charlene said, pulled her credit card from her purse, and waved it in the air.

"Name your price."

"Five thousand dollars," he said.

"Your sales clerk said five hundred," Charlene said, her voice heavy with indignation.

"I see," Mr. Heller began, "perhaps you do not wish to buy the necklace today. Perhaps it is not meant for you as Adira has stated."

Charlene was furious. *Stupid old fart is milking me for all he can,* she thought. *Well you're not going to win, you greedy, old man.*

"No, no, five thousand is fine," she said in the most pleasant tone she could muster. "I just thought since your clerk said five hundred, maybe there was a mistake."

"Adira sets her price, and I set mine," Mr. Heller said.

Charlene swallowed hard, forced a smile, and handed him her credit card.

"Please wrap the necklace well," she said, "and for that price, put it in a nice box, the nicest one you have."

"But of course," Mr. Heller said.

Charlene stood taping her foot, waiting for the necklace while Mr. Heller packaged it. Finally, he handed Charlene her coveted item, wrapped, boxed, and bagged. She was happy to have it, but annoyed the purchase had left her credit card maxed.

Charlene walked out of the store, the bag firmly in hand. She crossed the street and looked back. She noticed Adira in a window directly above the store watching her. Charlene waved at her and held up the bag with a smug look on her face. Adira shook her head and looked away.

Charlene put her nose in the air, and set off down the sidewalk, anxious to get home with her new prize.

***

Charlene unlocked the door to her apartment, closed it behind her, and removed the necklace from its wrappings. She went over to the table of items offered to Maehaem, and placed the necklace alongside a dagger with an ornate red handle.

Certainly this pendant must have great power, she thought. *The name alone, the Spiral of Blood, must give one power over one's enemies.* Charlene delighted in the idea.

She lit the candles on the table in honor of Maehaem as she did everyday, but today she had a special offering and hoped her Goddess would approve.

Charlene went to her desk to work. She was employed by an insurance company. When her mother had been ill, her employer allowed her to work from home. After her mother died, Charlene was grieving, and her employer allowed her to continue to work from home.

Charlene decided she liked working from home, and kept making excuses why she could not return to the office. Since she was one of their best employees, she knew they'd allow her to work from home indefinitely.

She occasionally got up to stretch her legs and would walk by the corner shrine to make sure the candles were burning safely it their glass jars. As she stood watching the flames of the candles, she thought about the necklace and wished she could have understood the sacred book. Her eyes fell upon the necklace, and again she felt its mysterious pull.

It was then the necklace slid off the table and fell to the floor. Charlene was astonished. The necklace had been securely placed on the table away from the edge. She lived alone and had no pets.

There's no way that could have just fallen off the table, she thought. *Maehaem must want me to wear it. That must be it.* She picked up the necklace and eagerly put it on.

Charlene began walking back to her desk when she felt a strong cramp in her abdomen. She doubled over in pain and made her way to the bathroom. There was blood in her underwear, and she assumed her monthly cycle had begun a bit early. She changed her underwear, put them in the bathroom sink, and turned on the water.

As the sink was filling, she looked in the bathroom mirror and noticed something red under her nose. She grabbed a tissue and attempted to wipe it away. Blood began gushing out of her nose, dripping into the water that was filling in the sink below. Charlene had never had a nose bleed and found it odd. She pinched her nose with the tissue, sat down on the toilet seat cover, and waited for the bleeding to subside.

After her nose stopped bleeding, she felt ill and went into the kitchen to make a cup of tea with lemon. She began cutting a lemon in half when her hand slipped, and the blade of the knife lacerated the skin on her finger.

"What the hell?" she said aloud and returned to the bathroom for a bandage.

No sooner had she finished bandaging her finger, she felt something warm on the inside of her leg. She looked down and noticed her kaki slacks were saturated with blood.

"Great," she groaned and took off her pants.

While she was cleaning up, she felt something tickling inside her ear. She took a cotton swab, put it inside her ear canal, and swabbed in a circular motion. When she pulled the cotton swab out it was covered in blood. She grew anxious.

Why am I bleeding like this? Charlene thought.

She suddenly felt sick to her stomach. She lifted the toilet seat and crouched down near the bowl. She felt blood trickling out of her ear and down the side of her face as her stomach churned. She vomited into the toilet and the water turned red. She slammed the toilet seat down and flushed away the bloody water, her hands shaking.

Extremely anxious, Charlene phoned the doctor and demanded an emergency appointment.

Something must be terribly wrong, she thought. *What if it it's cancer?*

***

Charlene sat impatiently on the examining table waiting for Dr. Gifford to return. He had examined her thoroughly and took vials full of her blood. What she couldn't understand was why she was no longer bleeding anywhere. She thought at least her period, albeit early, should have still been present.

She had told Dr. Gifford about the blood from her nose, ear, and vomit, along with her early menstruation. She sensed he didn't believe her, which added to her frustration.

Dr. Gifford entered the room with a perplexed look on his aging face. His readers sat on the tip of his nose, and his brow furrowed as his steel-blue eyes studied his tablet. He sat on a stool near the examining table and looked up at Charlene.

"Well, Charlene, all your blood work checks out, and I can't find anything out of the ordinary with your physical examination. Your blood pressure is fine, heart sounds good, lungs are clear, and your pelvic exam appears normal," Dr. Gifford stated.

"Are you sure I don't have cancer?" Charlene asked.

"There is nothing I can find in my examination, or in your lab results, that would indicate a malignancy, Charlene."

"So why am bleeding like this?"

"You told my nurse you are not taking any herbal supplements, is that correct?"

"Yes."

"Alright," Dr. Gifford said as he typed notes on his electronic tablet. "I'm just double checking."

"Are you sure it isn't cancer? Perhaps you should refer me to a doctor who specializes in cancer."

"Why would I refer you to an oncologist, Charlene, when you don't have cancer?"

"Well, because an oncologist would be experienced in ruling out the possibility of cancer. You're just a general practitioner."

"I see," Dr. Gifford said as he continued to type. "Charlene, have you considered seeing a psychiatrist about your preoccupation with cancer? I know your mother died from the disease, and you took care of her. It's understandable that you'd have—"

"I don't need a shrink," Charlene interrupted. "What I need is a competent doctor."

"I see," Dr. Gifford said, cleared his throat, and resumed typing.

"You don't see anything," Charlene said, "and will you stop typing notes on that stupid thing?"

Dr. Gifford stopped typing and looked up at her over his readers.

"Yes, Charlene, what is it?"

"I have cancer," Charlene began, "and I need treatment. Will you please give me a referral? My insurance won't cover the cost if I don't have a referral."

"Most insurance companies require a referral," Dr. Gifford replied. He looked at Charlene to see if she was going to say anything else. When she didn't, he began typing again.

"Of course, Charlene, I will give you a referral if you insist," Dr. Gifford said when he'd finished typing.

"Yes, I insist," Charlene said with her nose in the air, eyebrows raised, and mouth returning to its usual pout.

"Very well," Dr. Gifford said as he stood up. "Why don't you get dressed and then see my nurse. She will have your referral."

He gave Charlene a polite nod and left the room.

Charlene dress and hurried to Dr. Gifford's nurse's station to obtain her referral. She was relieved that Dr. Gifford had come around. He had been her primary care physician for years, but she thought maybe he was getting a bit too old as he seemed not to recognize the symptoms of cancer when he encountered them.

Charlene arrived at the nurse's station, pushed past an elderly couple who stood waiting for a nurse, and cleared her throat loudly.

Dr. Gifford's nurse was a corpulent woman with a plump face. She looked up, her eyebrows raised in question.

"Yes, my name is Charlene Hubris. Dr. Gifford said you'd have my referral. I'm in need of an oncologist."

"I have your referral, Ms. Hubris, but it's not for an oncologist," the nurse said.

"What? Well, then what kind of doctor is it for?" Charlene asked.

"A psychiatrist," the nurse responded.

Charlene's jaw clenched and her face grew hot.

"Could you give Dr. Gifford a message for me?" Charlene asked the nurse in a tone deliberately meant to conceal her anger.

"Certainly," the nurse responded. She reached for a pad of paper and a pen. "What is the message?"

"Tell Dr. Gifford he is an incompetent, arrogant ass, and he will be hearing from my lawyer," Charlene said, tilted her head back, and looked down her nose at the nurse.

The nurse cleared her throat, wrote down what Charlene had said, and looked back at her.

"Is that all, Ms. Hubris?"

Charlene nodded as she glared at the nurse. She was annoyed the nurse did not seem to be the least bit fazed by her statement.

"Very well then," the nurse said, "here is your much needed referral."

The nurse handed Charlene the referral card with the name and telephone number of a psychiatrist.

Charlene silently raged as she forced a polite smile.

"Can I borrow your pen for a moment?" Charlene asked, as she took the card.

"Certainly," the nurse said and handed Charlene the pen.

Charlene took the pen and wrote on the back of the card. She handed it to the nurse and put the pen in her bag.

The nurse took the card and looked at the back of it.

It read: *Lose some weight, you fat ass!*

The nurse gasped and looked up at Charlene, who smirked back at her.

Charlene whipped her head in victory as she turned and walked towards the elevators. She entered an empty elevator and pushed the button to descend to the parking lot.

"Nobody messes with me," Charlene whispered, "isn't that right, Maehaem? I have cancer and they think it's a joke and refer me to a shrink. They are putting my life in jeopardy. Without a referral how will I afford treatment? Maehaem, make them pay for their careless treatment of me."

***

Charlene arrived at home with a splitting headache. She was unable to work and needed to lie down. She went into the bathroom, opened the medicine chest, and retrieved the prescription medication she took for severe headaches.

She filled a glass with water and swallowed two of the headache tablets. She then grabbed the bottle of sleeping pills, opened it, shook some of the pills into her hand, and washed them down with the remaining water in the glass.

She felt a tickle in her throat and started coughing. She wondered if one of the pills had become lodged in her throat because she couldn't stop coughing. She coughed up something and spit into the bathroom sink. It was blood.

Is the cancer in my lungs? Charlene thought.

She got a tissue and blew her nose. Blood saturated the tissue. Charlene grabbed the tissue box and headed for her bedroom. The bleeding frightened her, but the headache was unbearable. She needed to lie down and sleep.

She crawled into bed and pulled the covers up under her chin. She was just nodding off when the phone rang.

"Hello?" Charlene said.

"Hey Char, are you working, or do you have a minute to chat?" asked a woman's voice.

It was Sheila, her latest friend. They had met in a candle shop six months prior and struck up a conversation. They had a lot in common, and since Charlene was without a friend at the time, she thought Sheila would do.

"Sheila, this isn't a good time," Charlene responded. "I've just come from the doctor's office. I am quite ill, and I need to rest."

"Oh wow, Char, sorry to hear that. Is it the flu or something?"

Charlene hated the way Sheila called her *Char*. She thought Sheila was nice, but a bit stupid and often annoying.

"No, it is not the flu," Charlene sighed. "I have cancer, Sheila."

"Oh my God, Char, I'm so sorry. What kind?"

Charlene thought about her response. She didn't know what kind, but was certain it was serious.

"I can't remember the name, it's complicated, but it has to do with the blood," she replied.

"Oh wow, Char, are you going to have to take chemotherapy or something?"

"Probably, Sheila, I don't know. All I know is right now my head is splitting, and I need to sleep."

"Oh, right. Sorry, Char. Call me later," Shelia said.

Charlene disconnected the call without saying goodbye.

Yeah right, she thought. *I'll call you later and listen to your stupid, 'Oh wow, Char' crap.*

She fluffed her pillows and closed her eyes. She felt the necklace around her neck. She clasped her hand around the pendant and fell asleep.

***

Charlene found herself in Heller's antique store. Adira was standing behind the glass counter with the sacred book in her hand. She was scowling at Charlene and shaking her head.

"What's your problem?" Charlene asked.

"You are the one with the problem, no? Is that not why you have come?" Adira responded.

"Well, yes, but you can't help me. I have cancer, and my doctor is too stupid to recognize it. He won't help me, or give me a referral to a doctor who can treat me."

"You don't have cancer, you foolish woman. You are not destined to own the Spiral of Blood, and because you possess it without destiny, you have now entered it."

"Entered what?" Charlene asked.

"The Spiral of Blood, of course," Adria replied.

"How could I enter the pendant?"

"You foolish woman, you have not entered the pendant. You have entered *The* Spiral of Blood."

Charlene felt sick. "You mean that's why I've been having all these bleeding episodes?"

"Yes and the bleeding will come again and again, until you have no blood left. Those who are not destined to own the sacred Spiral of Blood pendant are cursed to enter it. This is your fate."

"Why didn't you tell me that's what would happen when I wanted to buy it, you crackpot Gypsy?"

"You are a rude woman. You insult me and my people. I tried to tell you, but you would not listen. You could not read the sacred book of my ancestors, and you knew you could not."

"Then it's that old man's fault. He charged me five thousand dollars for the necklace. Did he know what it would do?"

"No, he does not know. He does not believe in such things, and it is not his fault. You are the one who has brought the curse of the Spiral of Blood upon you. The blame lies with you."

"What the hell am I suppose to do about it now?" Charlene asked. "How about I return it, and the old man can give me my money back? Will that stop the curse?"

Adira shook her head. "Returning the necklace will not stop the curse. Besides, at Heller Antiques, all sales are final."

Adria let out a mirthless laugh that seemed to pierce Charlene's head like a spear. She continued to laugh while staring at Charlene, her laughter becoming louder and louder.

"Shut up you stupid bitch, and tell me what to do!"

Adria stopped laughing and offered Charlene a menacing grin before a grave expression washed over her face.

"Examine your skin," Adira said. "If the Spiral of Blood is visible anywhere on your body, the time is upon you. Call to Maehaem. She will release you."

***

Charlene woke with a start, sat up, and drew a long breath. She looked around the room and realized she had been dreaming.

"It's just a dream," she whispered as she reached for her slippers. She sat on the edge of the bed thinking about the dream.

What had Adria said – something about checking my skin for the Spiral of Blood? And asking Maehaem for help…yes, that was it. Adria said Maehaem would release me. She must have meant from the curse.

Charlene stood up and began examining at her skin. She looked her arms and legs, but saw nothing. She unbuttoned her blouse to examine her chest. She saw a red spiral between her breasts, just above her bra. It looked exactly like the spiral on the pendant. She put the fingers of her left hand over the spiral and felt her heart beating. She felt it beat faster as her fear rose.

"Maehaem," she shouted. "I implore thee, release me!"

She sat down on the bed, now trembling with fear. The room grew cold and appeared to be filling with a blood-red fog. Charlene had the feeling she was no longer alone.

She turned her head and there stood a large, dark figure. It had wings like an angel that were black as coal. It had the head of a raven, and eyes that were gold and sparkled. Its body was that of a nude woman with dark skin. She wore snakes coiled around her wrists and ankles like bracelets and anklets. Her hands were huge, and her fingernails were long and sharp like razors. In her navel was a red gem that glowed.

"Maehaem, is that you?" Charlene asked, her entire body shaking with fear.

The bird woman opened her beak. Charlene heard a screeching sound with her ears, but the sound became a voice in her mind. The tone was angry and contemptuous.

"You think you know me. You think you are chosen by me. You build a shrine to honor me, and yet you have to ask if it is me?" the bird woman said.

Charlene felt shame and fear mix together and flow through her veins. She looked upon the bird woman and tried to open her mouth to offer an apology or ask for forgiveness, yet no words could she utter.

"You have asked me to release you from the Spiral of Blood curse. Is this your will?" the bird woman asked.

Charlene hesitated, fearing she would not be able to speak.

"Yes," she uttered and then nodded at the bird woman.

"Remove the Spiral of Blood pendant. Then lie down and close your eyes," the bird woman instructed.

Charlene swung her feet up on the bed. Her hands trembled as she removed the necklace and placed it on the bedside table. She reclined and closed her eyes, her heart pounding.

She felt a sharp, searing pain in her chest, right where the Spiral of Blood had been on her skin. She gasped for breath as she opened her eyes. She saw one of the huge hands with razor-like nails cutting open her chest, while the other hand reached in and cracked her sternum apart. The hands then stretched the opening wide to expose her beating heart.

Charlene tried to scream, but she was powerless to make any noise at all. The bird woman then made an odd bird-like call which summoned the ornate red handled dagger. It flew threw the air like an arrow aimed at Charlene's chest. The bird woman held Charlene's chest open with both her enormous hands, and the dagger plunged itself into Charlene's heart.

The bird woman then pulled her hands away. Charlene saw the ornate red handle of the dagger sticking out of her chest, quivering with each beat of her heart. She saw her white lace bra saturated with blood, and she felt her life ebbing away with each quivering beat.

Charlene looked around the room. She could no longer see the bird woman anywhere, but still sensed her presence. Her eyes darted to the bedside table. The necklace was gone.

Charlene had thought was special. She had thought she was gifted. She had thought she was chosen. She had thought she knew Maehaem, but realized she was wrong. She realized she was wrong about a lot of things.

Charlene's consciousness was fading when the words of the bird woman entered her mind.

"You are no more special than anyone else who venerates me. Your arrogance brought upon you a curse as it was I, Maehaem, who tested you with the Spiral of Blood pendant, and you failed. You angered me and encountered my darkest side this day. You have been released from the Spiral of Blood as you requested. Cross over in peace."

Charlene drew her last breath. The ornate red handle of the dagger ceased to quiver.

***

For three days Sheila tried telephoning Charlene with no response. She went to her apartment and knocked on Charlene's door. There was no answer. Fearful something had happened to her friend, she went to the apartment manager's office.

She told the manager her friend was not answering her phone or the door, and had just been diagnosed with cancer. She asked to be let in to Charlene's apartment to check on her.

The woman accompanied Sheila up to Charlene's apartment, and with keys in hand, opened the door.

Sheila entered first calling Charlene's name. The apartment smelled horrible. Sheila thought maybe Charlene had gone away for a few days and left trash in the kitchen bin. As she headed toward the back of the apartment where Charlene's bedroom was, the odor became revolting causing her to retch.

Shelia turned back and looked at the woman from the office that had let her in. The woman was standing in the kitchen, covering her nose and mouth with her hand. Sheila proceeded to Charlene's bedroom, also covering her nose and mouth. She opened the door, and a wave of the order hit her.

"Oh God, what the…" she said from under her hand.

"What is it?" the woman from the office asked.

"Something bad, something real bad, it smells awful," Shelia responded as she reached for the light switch.

Sheila flipped the switch and saw Charlene in her bed under the covers. It appeared as if she were sleeping. The smell told Sheila otherwise, but she could see nothing that would indicate why her friend was dead.

The odor overwhelmed Shelia, and she backed out of the room. She gagged a few times as she walked out to the kitchen and opened a window. She took a breath of fresh air and gathered herself.

The woman from the office stood looking at her.

"She's dead, isn't she?" the woman asked.

"I think so," Sheila replied. "She looks like she's just sleeping, but that smell."

She's dead. I've had this happen before with elderly tenants. I know that smell. I'll call the police," the woman said.

Sheila looked at the woman, and the reality of it hit her. The color drained from her face.

"Sit down, you've had a terrible shock," the woman said as she pulled out a table chair for Sheila to sit.

"I didn't know she was that sick," Shelia said.

The woman called the police and within a few hours, Charlene's body was on the way to the morgue. The woman from the office said she would contact Charlene's next of kin. Sheila asked the woman to give Charlene's family her name and phone number so she could be notified when the service for her friend would be held.

***

Charlene was buried next to her mother. Sheila attended the service as did Charlene's father and brother. There were a few people from the insurance agency where Charlene worked also in attendance. It was a small gathering.

Sheila approached Charlene's father after the service to introduce herself.

"Hi, I'm Sheila Dimard, Charlene's friend. We spoke on the phone," she said extending her hand.

"Nice to meet you, Sheila, I'm John Hubris, Charlene's father," the stout man said as he shook Sheila's hand.

"I'm so sorry for your loss," Sheila said. "I just learned of Charlene's cancer the day before she died."

"Thank you for your condolences," John replied, "but Charlene didn't have cancer."

"Charlene told me that she had cancer, over the phone, the last time we spoke," Sheila said.

"Dr. Gifford said he gave Charlene a clean bill of physical health the day before her passing. He said he was concerned about her mental health, though."

"Why?" Sheila asked.

"It seems she was obsessed with getting cancer, probably because her mother died of the disease. Apparently Charlene believed she had it despite no medical evidence. She told Dr. Gifford she was bleeding, but he told me he saw no evidence of that. He said he was concerned she might be suffering from a psychological disorder that and required treatment, and he referred her to a psychiatrist," John explained.

"She didn't mention that when we spoke on the phone."

"No, I don't imagine she would have," John said. "Since she was only thirty-nine, an autopsy was preformed. They told me it was standard procedure given the circumstances."

- 48 -

"Did they find out why she died?" Sheila asked.

John closed his eyes and took a long, deep breath.

"Oh God, I'm sorry. How insensitive of me," Sheila said.

"No, that's alright. It makes sense you'd want to know what caused your friend's death," John replied.

Sheila nodded.

"The pathologist said her heart stopped."

"She had a heart attack?" Shelia asked looking perplexed.

"No, they didn't say that," John replied, shaking his head. "They are still waiting on the toxicology report, but they think Charlene may have taken too many sleeping pills along with the prescription medication she took for headaches."

"Do you think it was an accident, or do you think she…" Shelia's voice trailed off when she saw the look on John's face.

John shrugged his shoulders. He gazed at his feet and lightly kicked the sod with the toe of his shoe. His mouth turned downward.

"In the past I'd have said there's no way Charlene would take too many pills on purpose," John said in a soft voice, "but after hearing what Dr. Gifford said about Charlene state of mind, well…I just don't know."

Forgotten

She found stillness in the wind of the storm that raged within and without. Blood red wine poured into a crystal glass, an offering to the demon demanding payment.

With death she danced yet again. The steps and rhythm she knew so well. Spinning, twirling, keeping time as it kept her, holding her hostage in a mind that rarely found stillness in the storm.

The eternal winds of the storm threatened to rage and blow away everything she knew. She embraced the possibility and closed her eyes to sleep. As fate would have it she would wake in the morrow to find death had forgotten her once more.

Miss Bitter

Miss Bitter was an old maid in the making, at least that's what Momma said. I asked her what an old maid was, but she didn't answer. Momma went on about Miss Bitter, telling me I should mind that I never become as self-absorbed as Miss Bitter.

"She thinks of no one but herself," Momma said, "and that is exactly why no man will ever want her. Why, what kind of a man would want a woman who can think of no one's feelings but her own?"

"I don't know, Momma, what kind of man?"

"No kind of man, Child. That is what I'm sayin'. Good Lord, do you listen to what I say?"

"Yes Momma, I was listenin', but I don't understand."

"What's not to understand? The woman is spiteful. Why, just look at her face. Do you know she's younger than your Momma? She don't look it though do she?"

I didn't think Momma looked old at all. I didn't think Miss Bitter looked old either, but her face was hard like stone. Maybe that's what Momma meant by looking old, having a face that looked like it was made of stone.

"I guess she don't, Momma."

"That's right, Child, she don't. She looks older than her years due to her spite. That kind of thing will shrivel up your heart and eat you from the inside out."

I thought about Miss Bitter's heart all shriveled up with teeth sticking out of it, eating her insides. Maybe that's why she looked like she did, because it hurt.

"She's not an attractive woman to begin with, not that I'm judgin' her on looks, mind you," Momma said as she grabbed another potato and started peeling.

"But when a woman don't have a pretty face, she best have a pretty heart."

I watched Momma peel the skin off the potato and grab another.

"Child, fetch me that pot in the cupboard so I cook these potatoes for supper."

I climbed down off the stool and got the pot Momma wanted. It was heavy, and I tried to put it on the counter, but I couldn't reach.

"Momma, I can't reach."

"Goodness, Child, give me that," Momma said, taking the pot and placing it on the counter.

As Momma cut the potatoes over the pot, one spit potato juice on her face. She laughed and wiped her face with her apron.

"When I finish peelin' these potatoes, Child, I'm gonna make a couple of apple pies for desert. Your daddy likes my apple pies, he sure does."

"I likes 'em too, Momma."

"I know you do, Child, and you can have some after supper as long as you clean your plate."

I helped Momma finish the potatoes. She said I'm too young to use a knife, but she said I help by throwing the peels in the rubbish.

I thought about the apple pies Momma was going to make for desert. I hoped I could eat all my supper so I could have some. I thought about Miss Bitter too. I wondered what her face would look like if she ate some of Momma's apple pie. Maybe it wouldn't look like stone no more. Maybe she'd smile, and her heart wouldn't hurt.

"Momma, do you think if Miss Bitter had some of your apple pie, it might help?"

"That's awful sweet of you to think of Miss Bitter, Child, but I think the only kind of apple that would help her is the kind in that movie, *Snow White and the Seven Dwarfs*."

"But Momma, that apple was poisoned by the Evil Queen! She was trying to kill Snow White."

"That's true, Child, but she don't die, do she? No, she don't. She falls into a sleep so deep that the dwarfs think she's dead, and they put her in a glass coffin, remember?"

"Yes, Momma, I remember."

Momma and I watched that movie once. It was alright, but I didn't like it much, and I wasn't sad to see it go back to the library.

"And in the end a handsome prince kisses her, and she wakes to find true love and gets married," Momma said.

"So Miss Bitter needs a handsome prince to kiss her to find true love and get married?"

Momma laughed. "What I mean to say is the only thing that will help Miss Bitter is if she finds true love, the kind that lasts a lifetime."

"Just like Snow White did?"

"Well, I suppose so, yes," Momma said, "but as I said, Miss Bitter is an old maid in the makin'."

"Momma, what is an old maid?"

"Didn't I already tell you that, Child?"

I shook my head.

An old maid is a woman who has never married."

"Like Miss Bitter?"

"Yes, like Miss Bitter. Of course, she could find true love and marry. Her days aren't done yet, the Good Lord willin'."

"How do we know she never found true love, Momma?"

"Well, we don't know for sure. All we know is she has never married. We can only guess she's never found true love. Most women who find true love get married."

"Maybe she don't wanna get married."

Momma threw her head back and laughed. "Well, Child, you may be right. These days' women don't worry much about becomin' an old maid. Times have changed."

I thought about Miss Bitter eating some of Momma's apple pie again.

"Momma, may I go next door to bring Miss Bitter a piece of your apple pie after dinner? It'll still be light out, and I promise to be careful. I won't stay long. You know Ms. Bitter don't like visitors any how."

"Why do you want to do that?" Momma asked.

"Maybe it will make her happy, and she might find true love and not become an old maid."

"You really think so, Child? You think my apple pie can make somebody happy?"

"Well, it always makes Daddy happy."

"That it does," Momma said. "Alright then, if you really want to, I don't see any harm in it. Now run along and play, Child, I need to start makin' the pies."

***

I went outside to play like Momma said. I saw Miss Bitter at her mail box shuffling through her mail. She looked over at me and scowled.

"Mind your business," Miss Bitter said. "No one likes a nosy child."

Miss Bitter turned on her heel and strode off, turning to look back twice, both times with a sour look on her stone face.

I tried to imagine Miss Bitter eating some of Momma's apple pie with that stone, sour face of hers. Maybe Momma was right. Maybe Miss Bitter was an old maid in the making. Maybe one piece of pie wasn't going to work. Maybe she needed more.

I went over to the kitchen window and peeked in. Momma was making the apple pies. I sat down in the flower bed and thought about how I could give Miss Bitter more pie. Momma said I could give Miss Bitter a piece. I wondered if she'd be mad if I gave her a whole pie.

I thought about Ms. Bitter and Momma's apple pie so much it made me tired, so I took a nap in the flower bed. When I woke up, I peaked in the window. I didn't see Momma in the kitchen no more and the pies were on the cooling rack. I went around to the back door.

The pies smelled good. I got a box from the cupboard and put one of the pies in it. I snuck out of the house and went next door to Miss Bitter's house. I rang the door bell. Miss Bitter came to the door looking sour.

"Afternoon, Miss Bitter. I brought you one of my Momma's apple pies."

"Why on earth would you do that?" Miss Bitter asked, looking annoyed. "Did you put poison in it or something?"

Poison—I didn't know why Miss Bitter would think that. Unless…she knew the story about Snow White too!

"No, there's no poison in it, Miss Bitter. Do you think it would help?"

The look that came over Miss Bitter's face was like a storm rolling in off the sea. I thought her stone face might crack and crumble into pieces.

"You're an ignorant little child, ignorant and intolerable. The only way poison in that pie would help is if you ate it!"

"But Miss Bitter, I'm a boy."

Miss Bitter looked at me, confusion all over her stone face.

"What difference does that make?"

"Boys aren't old maids in the makin'."

"What?" Miss Bitter asked, looking shocked.

"I said, boys aren't—"

"I heard what you said!" Miss Bitter yelled. "You are an ignorant and disrespectful little brat. Get out of my sight, and don't let me lay eyes on you again until you're ready to apologize for being so rude."

Miss Bitter slammed the door real hard, and it almost knocked Momma's pie out of my hands.

I walked home with the pie thinking about Miss Bitter. She was in an awfully bad way. Her heart must hurt real bad to make her so mean. If she didn't find true love soon, there might be no hope for her.

***

The next day the door bell rang. Momma came out from the kitchen and answered it. It was Mrs. Molter from down the street.

"Ida, did you hear what happened to Miss Bitter?" Mrs. Molter asked.

"No, I didn't," Momma said. "Why, what happened?"

Mrs. Molter looked at me and then looked back at Momma.

"Go outside and play, Child. I need to talk to Mrs. Molter for a bit," Momma said.

I left the room, but I didn't go outside like Momma told me to. I went to the back door, opened it, and slammed it shut. Then I snuck back to the pallor and hid behind the sofa so Momma couldn't see. I listened to Momma and Mrs. Molter talking.

"Oh, sweet Jesus," Momma said, "that's terrible."

"Yes, it is," Mrs. Molter replied. "They don't know what the cause is just yet, but from what I've heard, she died a horribly painful death."

Miss Bitter was dead? I didn't understand.

Mrs. Molter and Momma talked some more, but I didn't listen. I was too busy thinking about Miss Bitter.

I heard the front door shut when Mrs. Molter left. Then I heard Momma walk back to the kitchen. I sat behind the sofa for a while longer trying to figure out what happened to Miss Bitter.

I thought Momma might know what happened. I wanted to ask her, but she was going to be awful mad when she found out I had been in the cellar. I wasn't allowed down there, at least not by myself. Daddy kept his tools in the cellar, and other stuff I wasn't allowed to touch.

I got up and went into the kitchen. Momma was drying the dishes. She looked over at me.

"What on earth is eatin' you, Child?"

"I heard what Mrs. Molter said about Miss Bitter."

"Good Lord, Child, I told you to go outside."

"I know, Momma. I'm sorry."

"That was nothin' for a child to hear. It's a terrible thing about Miss Bitter."

"I don't understand, Momma."

"Well, Child, people die. That's part of life. We're all only here until the Good Lord calls us home."

"That wasn't supposed to happen, Momma. The Good Lord wasn't supposed to call Miss Bitter home."

Momma looked at me with her serious face.

"Why do you say that, Child?"

"Well, Miss Bitter was supposed to fall asleep and a handsome prince was supposed to kiss her, and when she woke up she'd find true love. Then she'd get married and not become an old maid. She'd be happy and her face wouldn't look like stone anymore. She wouldn't scowl at me and look sour."

Momma shook her head and looked confused. Then her eyebrows got all squished up.

"What are you talkin' about, Child?"

"Well, you remember last night after supper when you wondered where one of your pies had gotten off to?"

"Yes, and you fessed up and told me you brought a whole pie over to Miss Bitter before supper."

"That's true, Momma, I did, but she got mad at somethin' I said, and she called me rude. She said she didn't want to lay eyes on me until I apologized, and then she slammed the door, so I brought the pie back home."

"Alright then, so why was the pie still missin'?"

"Well, I thought I best make amends to Miss Bitter since I insulted her. So I thought I'd take the pie back and say I was sorry, but I wanted the pie to be extra special so it would help Miss Bitter. She was in an awfully bad way, Momma, with her heart hurtin' and all."

"Go on, Child."

"So before I brought the pie back over, I went down in the cellar and —"

"You are not allowed in that cellar, Child!"

"I know Momma. I know you're mad, but I'm tryin' to figure out why Miss Bitter's handsome prince didn't come to kiss her and wake up so she could find true love and get married. Do you think it's because she didn't have dwarfs to put her in a glass coffin?"

"What?" Momma asked, and her eye brows squished up again. "A glass coffin — Child, what on earth are you talkin' about? And what were you doin' in that cellar anyhow?"

"I had to go in the cellar, Momma, to get that white powder Daddy keeps down there. I had to sprinkle it on the pie I gave to Miss Bitter. "

"You did what?" Momma asked her eyes opened wide. She looked like she was scared.

"I said I had to get that white powder and sprinkle —"

"That white powder is poison your Daddy uses to kill the rats that come 'round," Momma interrupted, and her face grew pale as paste.

"You put that on the pie you gave to Miss Bitter?"

"Yes, Momma, I had to. I didn't know how else to make the apples work. I don't know any magic spells. After Miss Bitter ate the pie, she was supposed fall asleep and be woken up by a kiss from a handsome prince."

Momma's face looked like she'd seen a ghost. She walked over to the kitchen table, pulled out a chair, and sat down.

"You mean like in that fairy tale movie *Snow White and the Seven Dwarfs* we watched that time and talked about yesterday while peelin' potatoes?" Momma asked.

"Yes, Momma, just like that, but it didn't work."

"Sweet Jesus in heaven, Child, sweet Jesus in heaven."

Momma put her face in her hands and kept talking to Jesus. I think she was praying for Miss Bitter's soul.

Poor Miss Bitter, her handsome prince never came to wake her up. I don't know why. I don't think Momma knew why either.

Eternally Yours: Notes from the Departed

It is with the deepest regret that I put my hand to paper and craft my fate with ink. The months since your passing have been unbearable. You were taken from me far too soon, and a large part of me has passed with you. I cannot remember how to live. I can only remember how to survive, and that is not enough.

The sun is not as bright nor the nights as peaceful. The roses in the garden have lost their sweet fragrance. Life has become tainted with a dark sorrow that has permeated my heart. The house is empty and cold. The memory of your voice whispers in our bed chamber, and I find it nearly impossible to place my head upon my pillow to sleep. How I long to be in your arms and feel your tender kiss upon my cheek when I wake. The harsh morning light reminds me my days shall never again be blessed with your beautiful smile or radiant presence.

I know it is a sin to do what I have planned, but if God in His infinite wisdom cannot understand my plight and have mercy on my soul, I know of no other who will. I cannot bear living without you another day. Since you draw breath no more, then no more shall I. The measure of eternity is nothing to the length of a single day without you.

Forgive me.

Eternally yours,
Edmund

Ambriel

To this day I've never experienced anything like it. I'm still not sure what to make of it. I guess you could say I had a near death experience. I didn't see the white light at the end of a tunnel people talk about, but I did see an angel.

As a kid I pictured angels to be like the Arch Angel Michael, a strong male figure with a sword ready to battle evil, or the cherub angels in paintings floating on clouds, or the white robed, gentle figures that were sent to deliver messages from God. What I saw that day wasn't like any angel I had ever imagined or seen in artwork.

My name is Larry Higgins, and I'm sixty-nine years old. My wife Mabel passed on a few years ago. I sure do miss her, God rest her soul. I thought the day *it* happened I would be reunited with Mabel, but it seems the man upstairs had other plans.

I was leaving work late one Thursday evening. I had to work overtime at the factory for that slave-driving boss of mine. I was tired, and I just wanted to go home, put my feet up, and have a few beers. I was in the parking lot putting my jacket and lunch box in my truck. (A lot of the fellas who worked at the plant bought their lunch from the pizza joint down the street. I tried it once, but the food bothered my stomach. Doc said at my age, and with my ulcer, I needed to watch what I ate. So I ate peanut butter and jelly sandwiches for lunch most days.)

I was looking for my keys in the pockets of my trousers, but I couldn't find them. I thought maybe I had left them in my jacket. My memory wasn't so good anymore. I reached into the truck to check my jacket, and while I was searching, a man came up behind me.

"Hey, old man," he said.

I pulled my head out of the truck and turned to look at him. He was a big man, tall, well over two hundred pounds, and a lot younger than me. Not real friendly looking either. I didn't recognize him, but I thought maybe he worked at the plant. A lot of the young fellas called me old man. Most gents my age were retired. I hoped to soon, but I couldn't afford to just yet.

"What can I do you for?" I asked.

He shoved me pretty hard, and I stumbled backwards into the side of the truck. It caught me off guard. I had no idea what this young fella's problem was, or why he had a bone to pick with me.

"You can do me for all the money you got, you old fart," he said.

I remember thinking, this can't be happening. I don't make shit for money, and it was the day before payday. I had about twenty bucks on me, if that.

I looked at him and thought he couldn't be too bright. After all, if you're going to rob somebody, wait until payday. His intelligence aside, it was clear he meant business, and more likely than not, things were going to get ugly.

Back in the day I would have been able to get a few good licks in even if I didn't win the fight. But now-a-days, I didn't stand much of a chance. I'm an old man with arthritis to boot. Not that I wouldn't give it a go if I had to, but I'd rather avoid it. Christ in heaven knows what a man his size could do to my old, aching bones.

"It's the day before payday," I said. "I only got about twenty bucks on me."

"That ain't shit," the man said, spit chewing tobacco on the ground, and pushed dirt over it with the toe of his boot.

"Well, like I said, it's the day before payday. Maybe you should pick someone else to rob."

"You think you're funny, old man?"

I remember wanting to ask him if he had a brain in his head, but I didn't. I just shook my head. In a situation like that, the last thing I was trying to be was funny.

"Give me your money, or I'll beat it out of you," he said, his eyes narrowing like an animal preparing to attack.

I braced myself. I reckoned it wasn't worth taking a beating to keep my twenty bucks, but that's all I had till the next day at quitting time when I got my check and could cash it. I had my heart set on buying a six pack of beer on the way home, and I wasn't about to give up my money just because some jackass thought he could pick on an old man.

"I don't think so, sonny," I said, "it's my money and you ain't got no right to it."

"Are you deaf, old man?"

"Well now I know you're stupid, because if I were deaf, I wouldn't be answering you, now would I?"

And that's when he punched me square in the noggin. I fell backwards and hit the ground, blood poured out of my nose, and down my face. Now, I'd taken a punch to the nose before, but I was a lot younger then. That punch nearly put my lights out.

As I lay there trying to get my bearings, the bastard was putting his hands in every pocket I had. While his hands were in my front pockets he got a little too close to my manhood and that set me off.

I pushed him hard in the chest, but he didn't move much. So I swung at the son of a bitch, and I hit him right where he'd hit me, but his nose didn't bleed like mine. Those damn blood thinners Doc's got me on make me bleed like a woman.

"You stupid, old waste of skin, give me your fuckin' money, or I will beat you to death."

It sort of amused me that he threatened my life. I'm nearly seventy and too broke to retire. I worked in a shit hole of a factory for lousy pay. Mabel was gone, and my dog Lucky died last week. The only thing I looked forward to was a few cold ones after work, and the day the Lord called me home to be with my Mabel again.

I looked at that man, that ignorant dung heap who was willing to beat me to steal a lousy twenty bucks, and I thought, maybe he was going to do me a favor by putting an end to it all.

"Well get to it, sonny, 'cause I ain't givin' you shit."

It seemed like a good idea at the time, but once those words were out of my mouth, and I saw the look in his eyes, I wasn't so sure.

He proceeded to give me a beating. It hurt, and I was scared. I'm not ashamed to admit it. I tried to defend myself as best I could, but it was pretty clear he was going to beat me to the point I'd be dead, or wish I were because I'd be so busted up. I felt like I might lose consciousness, and I thought, well Mabel, I'm coming home.

Then the sky turned a golden color I had never seen before. Right before I heard what sounded like thunder, I saw this big flash of what I thought was lightning, but now I'm not so sure it was. He hit me again, and my vision got all blurry.

When my vision cleared, I thought I must be dying. Before me stood a being not of this world, so I figured I was headed for the pearly gates. It looked like an angel, but there was no flowing white robe. She didn't appear to be the kind of angel that delivered a message from God or escorted you to heaven.

She wore no robes or clothing. She had the body of a goddess and enormous wings as white as a dove. She was extremely tall and carried the largest sword I had ever seen. Her face was beautiful, but it had the look of a warrior.

She quickly went to work. She grabbed the man who had been beating me by the waistband of his blue jeans, and with one hand she lifted him up off his feet.

I sat up and tried real hard to focus. I could see her lips moving, but I couldn't hear what she was saying. Then I noticed the ground beneath the man was wet. He'd gone and pissed himself which I found quite amusing.

Then she dropped him, and he fell like a rag doll. She bent over him, grabbed his head, and popped it off his neck like you'd pop the plastic top off a gallon of milk. Blood spurted everywhere and her dove-white wings looked as if they'd been speckled with red paint.

I sat frozen in fear. I remember thinking, what kind of angel is that? If it was an angel of death, then artwork of the grim reaper needed updating.

She took his decapitated head and put it between her hands. It crumbled into dust that fell to the ground and was swept away by the wind. She then went about ripping off his limbs, one by one, and turning them to dust. The last was his torso. That took her a few minutes longer, but dust it also became.

After she'd finished, she started coming towards me, and I feared I was next. She had that man's blood all over her, and I understood why her face resembled a warrior. As she got close to me, I remember thinking if I was going to die, the last thing I'd ever see was the loveliest pair of breasts God himself could have ever created, and in an odd way, there was comfort in that.

She looked at me and raised her eyebrows, as if she knew I was enjoying the sight of her womanly attributes. She started moving her lips again, and that's when I realized why I couldn't hear her before. She didn't speak words like you and I do. She spoke thoughts, and only the person she was speaking to could hear them in their head.

She told me her name was Ambriel.

I wanted to ask her if she was my guardian angel, but before I could open my mouth to speak the words, she was answering me.

She explained she was not my guardian angel. I had one, she said, and he watched over me, but the guardians didn't do what she did. She was a soul reaper.

I reckoned she could hear my thoughts too, but I'm used to speaking words when I talk to someone. She patiently waited for me to do so before answering.

"Are going to reap my soul too?" I asked her.

Ambriel explained she did not reap good souls, only bad ones, and since I wasn't a bad man, I had nothing to fear from her.

I was relieved. I didn't like the idea of having my head, arms, and legs ripped off, and turned to dust.

"Did my guardian angel send you?" I asked.

She explained my guardian angel had informed her I was in danger. She told me the man threatening my life was marked as a bad soul. She was sent to reap his soul, and in the process, save me. She explained my time was not up yet, but the man who had been beating me, his time was. Lucky for me, I guess.

Ambriel put her hands on me, and her thoughts told me not to be afraid. I felt a rush of something. I'm not sure what it was, but if felt similar to when I got a jolt of electricity the time I was fixing the wiring on Mabel's vacuum cleaner. At first it made me feel kind of sick, but then I felt a bit better, and my wounds stopped bleeding.

While Ambriel was healing me, I looked into her eyes, and I saw fire. There was no pupil, just a lovely green iris, and fire where a pupil should be. Her hair was light brown and short. It looked like silk. Her skin was luminous, and I couldn't help myself, I reached out and touched her arm. It felt soft, like velvet, but gave me a zap, sort of like sticking your finger in a light socket. I was in awe that something so beautiful could kill a man in the manner she had, and then heal another man just with her touch.

I wondered if soul reapers were healers too, but I didn't say it out loud. I just pondered it while looking at her.

She nodded her head. Then she told me soul reapers, like all angels, had the power to heal, but they didn't do it often. What they did most was reap souls.

Ambriel helped me to my feet, and when she did, well...I looked at her breasts again. They were right there in front of me. I may be an old man, but I'm still a man.

Ambriel asked me to look at her eyes not her breasts, or her thoughts asked. I felt my face flush. I felt like a school boy with a crush. Beautiful isn't strong enough of a word to describe what she was. Magnificent is closer, but even that fails to describe her glory.

She told me I would be fine, and that I should try to enjoy life more as my days weren't as short as I thought. She said Mabel was watching over me, and Lucky was still with me in the trailer, just in spirit now.

She told me she had to go, and then she smiled. The light that radiated from her smile was so brilliant, it was blinding. It was like looking into the sun. I squinted, trying to keep my eyes open, but I couldn't. I shut them and turned my head away. I felt her take my hand, put something in it, and gently close my fingers around it.

When I sensed the light had faded, and I opened my eyes. She was gone. She disappeared just as she had appeared, in the space of a heart beat. I opened my right hand and there were my keys.

I walked over to my truck and hopped in. I decided I wasn't going to get a six pack and go home after all. I was going to Murphy's pub, and have myself a good strong whiskey, maybe even two. Then I was going to ask that nice waitress who worked there if she'd like to go out to dinner on Saturday. She was a bit younger than me, just barely sixty years of age, but I intended to do what Ambriel suggested. I knew in my heart Mabel wouldn't mind.

Fallen

The sound of the bag pipes echoed in the stillness of the autumn afternoon. Solemn was the expression of every face in attendance.

The colors of the changing leaves were more vibrant than Terry ever remembered seeing them. The sky was the most beautiful and serene blue, yet this day full of nature's beauty was shadowed by sadness.

Terry kept his head bowed and his hands folded through most of the service. He wanted to remember Chris the way he was in life, not the way he found him that day on the battlefield.

Chris was a brave soldier. He was a loving husband and father. He was a good friend. He would forever be all those things, and he would forever be a hero.

They lowered him into his final place of rest. Tears fell and hearts were heavy. Time all but stopped for the heart that beat no more.

A Little Birdie Told Me

Dean woke to the sun streaming in the window. A smile spread across his face as he remembered the night before. To his right slept his beautiful new bride Mirabella. Dean was proud to have such a gorgeous woman as his wife. She was fifteen years his junior, and he thought she made him look good. His golfing buddies were envious. While they were all wealthy men, only Dean managed to marry a woman as beautiful and sensual as Mirabella.

Mirabella's face looked peaceful as she slept, and Dean decided not to wake her. They were on their honeymoon in a tropic paradise, and he wanted her well rested for all the indoor fun he had planned.

Dean slipped out of bed and dressed. He went over to the desk and pulled out a piece of the hotel's writing paper. He jotted a note to his new wife letting her know he'd gone to the café in the lobby for coffee and muffins. He placed the note on the bedside table and left.

When Dean returned to the room, he heard the shower running. He saw the note he had left for Mirabella now on the bed. He took the contents from the café out onto the balcony. It was a glorious view and a perfect place to have breakfast. He put the coffee and muffins on the table in the corner and sat down to read the newspaper he had picked up while in the lobby.

Meanwhile, Mirabella adjusted the tub faucet, trying to obtain a desirable temperature for a shower. It was either too hot or too cold, and she was quickly becoming frustrated.

"What the hell?" she grumbled as she fiddled with the faucet. "This is Dean's idea of a classy hotel?" she mused aloud before giving up and shutting the water off.

She decided to forgo the shower and looked around the bathroom for her robe.

Where the hell did I leave it? Mirabella thought.

Mirabella left the bathroom and searched the hotel room, but could not find it anywhere. Things had gotten pretty wild the night before, and clothing was strewn everywhere. She picked up the clothes it hopes of finding her robe. It was no where in sight, and she suspected Dean of hiding it.

I'm surprise he doesn't hide all my clothes so I'm nude all the time, just the way he likes me best, she thought.

Dean sat on the balcony reading the newspaper and sipping his coffee. A bird was chirping in a nearby tree, and it annoyed him. He looked up at a bird. It was a small song bird, what kind he didn't know, and he didn't care. He waved the newspaper at it in attempt to scare it off, but the bird stayed perched and continued twittering.

Dean was looking around for something he could throw at the bird when a call came in on his cell phone. He pulled the phone out of his pocket and looked to see who was calling. It was his secretary Kristine.

"Stupid bitch," he mumbled and let the call go to voice mail. He was tired of Kristine's clinging. They'd had a relationship, but it was purely sexual as far as he was concerned, and it happened before things got serious with Mirabella. All he wanted from Kristine now was for her to do what he paid her for. He had specifically told her no calls unless it was urgent. Dean figured she was probably calling with something trivial as an excuse to speak with him.

Women can be so pathetic, he thought.

As he sat brooding about Kristine's call, Mirabella stepped out onto the balcony. Much to Dean's surprise and delight, she was completely nude. Dean sat motionless as he watched Mirabella walk toward the railing and begin stretching. He thought her well-toned body was a sight to behold. The idea entered his head that Mirabella was unaware he was watching her, which added to his excitement.

Mirabella placed her hands on the railing. It was quite low, no more than a few feet high. It was short for a balcony five stories up, but it was an old resort, and the vintage architecture added to the charm.

Mirabella was an exquisite woman, one any man would be proud to call his wife, and Dean was indeed proud. He had insisted she take self-defense classes. She had balked at the suggestion, but he explained she was far too desirable of a woman not to know how to protect herself.

Dean believed Mirabella was the finest asset he possessed, and he had every intention of making sure she stayed that way. Now that she had mastered the self-defense classes, he planned on insisting on a cardio workout five times a week, as well as yoga classes to keep her ass in the shape that pleased him.

Mirabella leaned forward to look below. Dean continued to watch her. He wondered how long it would be before she realized he was there. With her hands still on the balcony railing, she looked up at the tree as the bird Dean had been watching started twittering again.

Mirabella looked at the bird curiously. It appeared as if were tweeting at her, and seemed unafraid she was within reach of it. She wondered if the little bird would allow her to touch it. She extended her arm upward, her fingers reaching, but the bird was just beyond her grasp. She went up on the balls of her feet it attempt to gain a few more inches, stretching as far as she could, but was unable to touch the little bird. She put her hands back on the railing and again peered over to look below, her dark hair falling forward around her face.

Dean found himself unable to control his desire to touch his wife's caramel-colored skin, and to posses her in every way he could possibly imagine. He approached her quietly. He thought the surprise would add to the excitement of the moment, which he envisioned as a passionate encounter right there on the balcony.

As far as Dean was concerned, a woman's main purpose was to gratify her man sexually. Mirabella knew this about Dean, and often felt she meant as much to him as his collection of expensive cars.

Dean unzipped the fly on his shorts. He planned to take his wife whether she was in the mood or not.

If she didn't want it, she should have kept her clothes on, he thought.

His shorts now down around his ankles, and Mirabella still leaning forward, Dean put a hand on each of his wife's shoulders. Mirabella gasped when Dean touched her, and he thought she found the surprise encounter as exciting as he did.

This is going to be fantastic, Dean thought, and pulled his wife against his body.

Mirabella never looked behind her. She was surprised how instinctually she responded when she took her hands from the railing and put them around Dean's wrists. She bent forward deeply, tucked her chin to her chest, pulled with all her strength, and propelled Dean's body over hers.

Dean might have been a bit sore, and his ego bruised, if Mirabella had not been standing so close to the railing. Instead he found himself being catapulted over the railing of the balcony, headed for the pavement five stories below.

Mirabella screamed his name as his body was hurtling towards the ground. Dean had planned on hearing his wife scream his name during their week in paradise, oh yes he had, however; he hadn't plan on hearing it *that* way.

Sadly for Dean, it was the last thing he would ever hear. More tragic was the last thing Dean would ever see: Mirabella, his beautiful new wife, smiling and waving as his body met the pavement.

Inside the hotel room, Mirabella's cell phone rang. She stood looking at Dean's lifeless body, and watched as blood seeped from underneath it, before going into the room to answer the phone.

She grabbed the phone, looked at the display, and smiled.

"It's done, baby, we're free," Mirabella said. "I can't wait to see you and show you how much I've missed you. We can finally be together, no more acting and no more Dean."

"How did you know everything was a go?" the voice on the other end of the call inquired.

Mirabella giggled in reply.

"The bastard let my call go to voice mail. That was the cue, remember? I call and tell Dean there was a problem with the Rendow account, and he'd bitch so loudly about me screwing it up that you'd know the will and life insurance papers were in order."

"Yes, Kris, I remember, that was the plan," Mirabella replied.

"So you just heard his phone ring and assumed it was me? That was risky, Bella."

"Actually, his phone vibrated," Mirabella said.

"You *heard* his phone vibrate?"

"No, I didn't."

"Then how the hell did you know?"

"Well," Mirabella began, "Dean looked at his phone, and he said, you stupid bitch, so I knew it was you calling, and the papers were in order."

"So you heard him then," Kristine said. "Why didn't you just say so, baby?"

"I didn't hear him," Mirabella laughed. "A little birdie told me."

Freedom's Price

She waited at the window everyday for him to come home. She never knew when he left if he would return safe and whole.

His job was an important one. It required he take life-threatening risks, and he did so each day he donned his uniform. It was the cost of freedom, and he believed it was worth it.

One day while waiting at the window as she always did, she watched the day fade, and darkness blanket the remaining daylight. She continued to wait, her impatience growing, and her worry building. She didn't see him. That night he didn't return safe and whole.

The next time she saw him, he lay in his coffin wearing his dress uniform and looking peaceful. His colorful medals now rested on a chest that was forever stilled. She kissed his forehead and whispered her goodbyes before his coffin was closed and draped with the American flag.

She watched as the vessel that encased his body was lowered into the ground. She received the flag that had draped his coffin, folded ever so carefully, into a triangle of remembrance.

It was the cost of freedom, and she wasn't sure it was worth it.

The Spirit of the Wolf

Every breath Cheyenne took hurt. Each movement of her diaphragm felt like being pierced with a knife. She wiped the tears from her face and noticed the black tinge of my mascara on her fingers.

So much for waterproof mascara, I must have raccoon eyes by now, she thought.

Cheyenne walked her battered body into the bathroom and over to the vanity. She reluctantly looked into the mirror. Not only were her eyes black from the smeared mascara, but they were darkening from the punch she'd taken to her nose.

"Surely by morning you'll look like a boxer who lost the fight," she whispered to her reflection.

She unbuttoned her blood stained blouse. She slipped it off her shoulders and winced from the pain. She let the blouse fall to the floor. Her arms were showing signs of bruising as well as the skin covering her ribs.

Perry really worked me over this time, the son of a bitch, she thought.

Her hands cupped the slight swelling protruding from below her navel.

His child is growing inside me, and he can't be bothered to avoid its home with his raging fists.

Cheyenne looked at her reflection again and felt ashamed. She hated herself for allowing it to continue. She knew she couldn't let him harm her unborn child. Even if it managed to survive to be born, she wouldn't allow him to show it his twisted version of love—a version that involved name calling, opened handed slaps, and closed fist contact.

Cheyenne's thoughts drifted to the future, and she saw herself holding a precious bundle of innocence. That same bundle was then being thrashed about during one of Perry's drunken rages as she tried desperately to hold on to it and keep it safe.

Her whole body shivered as she shook her mind from its twisted vision. She felt anger rise inside her, like poison traveling through her veins. She knew what she must do.

She walked into the living room where he kept his prize possession hanging on the wall. It was a sword, some silly movie replica he just had to have. She took it off the wall and examined the tip of the blade.

Movie replica or not, it's sharp enough to do the job. With any luck, it won't do it very well, and he'll suffer all the more for it, she thought, and a slight smile crept over her face.

She headed down the hallway towards the bedroom where Perry was passed out, sleeping off his latest bender. Her heart pounded in her chest with each step she took. She slowed her pace and tiptoed to the bedroom door.

She lifted the sword and looked at the blade. The soft glow of the hall nightlight reflected off its silver metal. She watched as the glimmer of light danced on the blade with the trembling of her hands.

If I don't get this right, he'll kill me for sure, she thought. *Either way, it is ending tonight.*

Cheyenne crept into the dimly lit bedroom. She saw Perry lying flat on his back, his beer belly rising and falling with his breath. She planned to plunge the sword into his chest and pierce his heart. She inched closer to the bed. She raised the sword over her head and readied herself when Perry opened his eyes and looked at her.

Cheyenne froze arms over her head, sword at the ready, her body growing numb and incapacitated by his glare.

Just do it! Do it now! Cheyenne thought, but found herself paralyzed with fear.

"What the fuck do you think you're doing?" Perry said his breath beer-laden and putrid.

Cheyenne didn't respond. She still couldn't move. She could barely breathe.

"And what hell are you doing with my sword? You think you're going to kill me with that thing, you dumb bitch?"

Perry started laughing.

He laughs because he always wins, Cheyenne thought. *What was I thinking?*

"You don't have the balls or the brains to take me out, you ditz," Perry grumbled as he started to move from his bender recovery position.

Cheyenne saw herself dead, fearing at any moment he would reach up, rip the sword from her hands, and slit her throat. Even if it was only a movie replica, she was sure it would cut her throat with enough force behind it.

"I asked what do you think you're doing, you ignorant douche bag," he demanded.

"I won't let you hurt me or my baby anymore," Cheyenne said her voice no more than a whisper, her heart pounding, her hands still shaking, yet her immobility easing.

"You won't *let* me?" he smirked. "Hey, do you want to know what a woman is?"

Cheyenne shook her head.

A disgusting grin grew on Perry's face. "A woman is a life support for a c—"

"Shut up!" Cheyenne screamed. "Shut your filthy mouth, you misogynistic pig!"

"Oh no, I'm sooo scared," Perry responded sarcastically. "Cheyenne's using big words because she's sooo smart."

Perry roared with laughter. He didn't seem at all concerned that Cheyenne had his sword in her hands, holding it over his chest.

Time seemed to slow as Perry laughed. Cheyenne wondered whose voice had said those words to Perry. She wondered if that voice really belonged to her. When she realized it did, she finally accepted how Perry saw her. For the first time fear left Cheyenne, and things became clear.

Cheyenne realized she wasn't a human being to Perry, and neither was her unborn child. She was simply a piece of ass, and the innocent life growing inside her, nothing more than a parasite.

That is how he sees us. That's all we are to him.

Cheyenne wasn't sure if it was Perry's incessant laughing that set her off, or perhaps it was the realization of what she meant to him, of what their baby meant to him that pushed her over the edge. She plunged the sword to the right of his head. Its metal tip ripped into the pillow upon which his head lay.

Perry stopped laughing and stared at Cheyenne. For the first time he had fear in his eyes, the same kind of fear he usually put in hers.

Cheyenne decided piercing Perry's heart was too good for him. She felt he deserved much worse. After drawing her conclusions about Perry's fate, she proceeded down a path that would cause her to question herself even more.

***

Although time had passed, Cheyenne never fully understood what had come over her that night. Not long after it happened, she met a woman who said it was the spirit of the wolf that had possessed her. Cheyenne thought perhaps the woman was right. She wasn't sure what else would have caused her to rip part of Perry's trachea from his throat with her teeth, spit it in his face, and then sit and listen to the sound of blood gurgling in the back of his throat as he died.

Cheyenne stood trial for Perry's demise. Not guilty was her plea, and self-defense was her claim. She had a good lawyer who said she had an excellent case.

"Cheyenne's actions were primal," her lawyer began, "which serve as a testament to how severely Perry had tormented her with his mental and physical abuse. She felt compelled to take such visceral action to defend herself," he concluded in his closing argument.

Not guilty were the words Cheyenne's lawyer was looking for, and he was most pleased to hear them. Cheyenne was glad she was free of the monster who had abused her, and relieved she would not have to give birth in prison.

***

Cheyenne's baby was due in a week. During her last ultrasound, she was told it was a boy. She finished decorating the nursery and asked her mother to drop by to see it.

"Wolves—I know you're having a boy, but to decorate a nursery with images of wolves?" Cheyenne's mother said after looking at the nursery.

"Yes, wolves," Cheyenne replied.

Her mother looked at her, a bit confused by her daughter's choice of decor, but simply smiled and nodded.

Cheyenne didn't try to explain. She thought perhaps no one would understand that in those images she was honoring the spirit of the wolf that had saved her and her unborn child from Perry's violence and abuse. She thought it was the least she could do for the spirit of an animal that seemed to possess her that fateful night, and guided her and her unborn son to freedom.

Whispers in the Wind

The October leaves rustled in her wake as she descended the stone steps of the old cemetery. Barren branches and leaf adorned paths led the way to an awaited reunion. The time had come, for the veil was thin.

The tombs of the departed marked the final resting place of souls who once drew breath. The dates of their deaths, etched in stone and granite, bore witness to the time they passed from the world of the living to the realm of the dead.

Her mood grew solemn as she approached the graves of her ancestors and placed glass jar candles upon their final resting place. She sat amongst the fallen leaves and looked up at the sky. The day was surrendering its light to the approaching darkness, just as life surrenders its breath to the transition of death.

She lit the candles in the glass jars and returned to her place amongst the leaves. She listened. The wind began to rustle the leaves and lifted them upward, whirling them about. She watched them dance and swirl around her as the candle light grew bolder.

Darkness consumed the day and twilight fell. She heard the howling of stronger winds coming forth. She closed her eyes and bowed her head. They had arrived.

The whispers in wind are the voices of the dead.

Tyler's Light

Tyler walked through the woods, the ground blanketed with autumn leaves. The vibrant colors of red, orange, and yellow embellished his path. The birch trees, with their white bark and grey markings, were like friends welcoming him to their home.

He looked for the large rock that marked the spot and headed towards it. As he walked he listened to the leaves crunching beneath his feet. He listened to the birds twittering in the trees. He listened to wind rustling the fallen leaves.

As he neared the large rock, he began looking for the flat stone he had used to mark her final resting place. His eyes fell upon it, and he crouched down to brush away the leaves and debris.

He put his right palm on the stone and closed his eyes. He thought of her running and playing. She loved to swim in the lake. She loved walks in the woods and often accompanied him.

Tyler pulled a photo out of his pocket, sat down, and crossed his legs. A black Labrador retriever sat in the photograph, tongue hanging out the side of her mouth. She wore a red collar, and a silver heart-shaped tag that read: *Lucy.*

Lucy had been his best friend and companion. She had been his partner in getting into mischief. She had been there when he woke from a bad dream to jump up on the bed, even though his mom said she was supposed to stay on the floor.

When Lucy got sick, Tyler's mom said she had to be put to sleep. She said it was best for Lucy. Tyler cried the day Lucy died. His mom told him the name Lucy meant light. It comforted Tyler to know that. Lucy had been a light in his life, and in a way, she always would be.

Tyler sat smiling thinking of his dog and how she loved to run through the woods in which he now sat. He knew he had done the right thing by burying her in the place she loved so much. His dad and he had to carry her, wrapped in an old blanket, the entire way. Tyler cried. His dad cried too, but Tyler pretended not to notice.

"I'll be back next weekend, Lucy, unless the weather's bad. I brought you a new ball," Tyler said.

He pulled a bright yellow tennis ball from his jacket pocket and placed it on the flat stone. He never knew what happened to all the tennis balls he brought and left on that stone. They were never anywhere to be found. He liked to think Lucy had them, even if that wasn't possible, he liked to think it.

The Circle of Life

"Does it really matter now?" he asked in a hushed tone. His voice — even when he spoke softly — was gold set in gravel.

He began telling me what he thought and felt the first time he ever saw me, the day we met in the park. I had heard the story several times before, but I never tired of it.

I closed my eyes imagined myself in the park on that beautiful spring day. I wished I could transport myself back there and relive meeting him all over again.

As he told our story, I drifted into the timbre of his voice, and into the decades of memories we'd made.

I could sense his eyes burning into me, but I dared not open mine. I wanted to stay in my self-created darkness of memories and listen to him talk.

"Even God can't help us now," he whispered.

I took a deep breath. I wanted to breathe the present moment away. I wanted to remember our past.

He kissed me on my forehead. I opened my eyes and looked into his. The intensity of his gaze envelope every fiber of my being and inscribed an unspoken message on my soul. It was a feeling I would never forget.

A brilliant light flashed and everything simply stopped. His eyes were no more. My thoughts ceased for what seemed an eternity.

***

I gathered my school books and stuffed them into my backpack. It was the first day back to school after summer break.

"Come on, you're late!" my mother called from the kitchen.

As I hurried down the stairs, I swung my backpack over my shoulder and accidentally knocked a picture of my great-grandfather off the wall. It tumbled a bit before coming to rest on one of the carpeted steps. I followed it down the few steps it had traveled and picked it up.

I had seen it before, but I had never paid much attention to it. As I looked it over to make sure the glass hadn't cracked in the fall, I noticed my great-grandfather's smile in the photo. I looked into his eyes and my stomach dropped.

"What are you doing?" my mother asked as she climbed the stairs to meet me.

"Mom, how did your grandfather die?"

"I told you, sweetheart, my grandfather died in the war."

"But you said he wasn't a solider."

"That's right."

"So how did he die in the war then?"

My mother took a deep breath and paused before responding.

"The town where my grandfather lived was bombed," my mother answered.

"Did your grandmother die with him?"

"Yes, dear, she did," my mother said, and she reached for another picture on the wall.

"See," my mother said as she handed me the framed photograph, "you have her eyes."

I looked at the photograph of my great-grandmother and saw my own eyes looking back at me. I handed the pictures of my deceased great-grandparents back to my mother and quickly descended the stairs.

If I'm here again, I thought, so is he.

Flat Soda

Saffron sat staring at the keyboard of her computer, its lettered keys worn from hours of typing. Sometimes her thoughts flowed so rapidly, her fingers could barley keep up, but not today. Today her fingers sat idle, the screen on the computer empty, her mind devoid of a creative thought.

"Writer's block," she grumbled.

She gave the keyboard a good shove for not clicking away like she knew it could. She rose from her chair and gave it a shove as well.

I might as well get some housework done, she thought. *It seems there isn't going to be any writing done today.*

The clothes flew across the floor as she sorted the laundry. The washing machine door received a good slam for its trouble of being stuffed full of dirty clothes. It had no choice. She would stuff those clothes in that washer, and it would take it until it could take no more. Then when the clothes didn't come as clean as they should have, she'd blame it for being a lousy machine, not herself for over loading it.

She went back to her computer and stared at the blank white screen as it stared back at her, waiting for her to fill it. She gave a heavy sigh of disgust, closed the writing program down, double clicked on her favorite icon, and was browsing the web in no time.

Surely doing some shopping will make me feel better, she thought.

She typed in her favorite search words and waited to see what she could buy that she most certainly didn't need. It was her favorite thing to do, or it used to be. It made her feel better even if only for a little while, but not today.

Nothing interested Saffron much anymore. Everything was flat—flat like a two liter bottle of soda that had the cap left off.

Maybe I'm depressed, she thought. *Maybe some pharmaceutical intervention is what I need.*

Saffron had lost her passion for most everything she was once passionate about. She felt tired, her head ached, and cheery she most certainly was not.

Flat soda, that's what I am, she thought.

She pushed the keyboard away once again, and turned in her chair to look out the window.

Flat soda is boring. It has no pep, no fizz. Flat soda doesn't taste good, and it gets poured down the drain.

Saffron turned back to her computer and pulled the keyboard towards her. She opened the word program and began to write. The hours passed as Saffron continued to type away, her fingers becoming cramped and her legs equally so.

Finally Saffron fatigued and decided to call it a day. She looked over her work and knew it was rough, but it was a start. She had filled several pages with something that was neither boring nor flat, that had pep, and didn't need to be poured down the drain.

It was then Saffron realized that perhaps flat soda had its benefits. Maybe flat soda was a muse that came in the guise of having interest and passion for nothing unless you created it. Maybe any state of mind had a purpose, even when it seemed it was of no use, even when it seemed it should be discarded, and even when it was uncomfortable.

"Saffy, I'm getting myself something to drink. Would you like a soda or iced tea?" Saffron's husband called from the kitchen upon returning home from work.

"Is the soda flat?" Saffron asked.

"Ah…well, the cap wasn't on tight, so it might be. You want iced tea instead?"

Saffron smiled. "No, that's okay, flat soda's fine."

Virginia and the Cat

I threw the manuscript on the floor. Reading it aloud was a lousy idea. I wondered why I took note of such advice. I couldn't stand the sight of it, never mind the sound of it. I swear I wrote it to torture myself, because that's what it did, and it did so quite well.

She looked at me with her glassy, green eyes, or perhaps she looked through me.

"What?" I asked. "What the hell are you looking at?"

I swiveled in my desk chair, turning my back to her.

You of course, she hissed. ***Are you really that stupid?***

The thought that I had heard her answer me crept into my mind, but I dismissed it as merely my imagination. After all, I hadn't slept in days.

"My mind is playing tricks on me. Yes, that's it, nothing more," I said.

No, that's not it, stupid.

I turned around and stared at her. My head ached as my mind swirled with plausible explanations for what I thought I heard. My breathing grew more rapid with each passing thought, and my heat rate increased as panic loomed.

I couldn't stay seated any longer. I went into the kitchen and paced, hoping to relieve the building tension. She followed me. She always followed me. That was one of the things that made her such a good companion. At least I thought it did.

She sauntered across the kitchen floor as if she hadn't a care in the world. She sat facing me in front of the French doors that overlooked the balcony.

I stopped pacing and looked at her. The moonlight reflected off her pewter colored fur, and her glassy, green eyes looked hypnotic yet sinister.

She turned and looked out the door at the moonlight for a few moments and then back at me.

Figure it out yet?

"I'm tired and imagining things. That's all it is, nothing more," I whispered in hopes of calming myself.

Are you sure about that, stupid?

Time seemed to slow, and then it seemed as if it had stopped, when suddenly it began to race and panic consumed me. My heart pounded in my chest, my stomach churned, and I felt as if I were suffocating. The terror was so great, death would have been mercy. I paced frantically, reciting prayers aloud, praying for the panic to cease, for the fear to just go away.

How utterly pathetic you are. What are you afraid of? Thoughts in your head, or is it my voice—is that what's got you in such a state? Scaredy-cat, scaredy-cat, scaredy-cat!

"Shut up!" I yelled before slapping my hand over my mouth.

Wake up the whole building why don't you? Tell them all what I already know. You're a big scaredy-cat and a stupid one at that!

Her voice sounded strange, similar to a human voice acting the role of a cartoon character. There was a slight accent as well. At times she rolled her R's like a Scotsman, while at others she dropped them like a Bostonian. It was most odd.

My heart was still racing, but the panic was fading as my focus shifted. I crouched down next to her, and she peered back at me with her glassy, green cat eyes.

"Cat's don't talk," I whispered to her.

I waited for a reply, but there was only silence. I shook my head and stood up.

"I knew it. I imagined the whole thing and scared the crap out of myself in the process," I said.

You didn't imagine it. I was listening when you read your manuscript out loud. Trust me, you're imagination isn't that good.

I looked at her. She glared at me. It was a staring match she would most certainly win if I gave her the chance. My imagination couldn't be that bad if I thought she was talking to me. It had to be my imagination, a result of severe fatigue, unless…it was something far more insidious.

"They're going to put me in one of those padded rooms for sure and load me up with a chemical cocktail until I drool in a corner all day," I said, looking at her.

Oh for Christ's sake, stop being so melodramatic. Why don't you just relax?

She yawned and stood up, her back arched as she stretched. She gave me what appeared to be a look of disgust and sauntered back into the other room. I followed her and watched as she sprawled out on the carpet. She turned her head and looked at me.

Have a seat. You don't look so good, stupid.

I sat down in my desk chair.

"Stop calling me stupid."

I would, but that's what you are.

"And you're a bitch. Oh Jesus, help me, I'm arguing with my cat."

She glared at me, her glassy, green eyes peering in to my soul.

Jesus can't help you. I can help you. Why don't you stop freaking out, and ask me what you want to know? That, of course, would be everything—right, stupid?

Stupid—since when did that become my name? And how big is the brain of a cat anyway?

She yawned, twitched her whiskers, and looked at me.

"Fine," I began, "Are you a demon in the body of a cat? You must be an evil creature or some spawn of the devil."

No, but would you feel better if I said yes?

She paused as if waiting for my response, but simply laughed. Her laughter was even more disturbing than her voice. It was a mocking laugh, cold and heartless.

If there was no demon in her, was this really my cat? It didn't make sense. My cat loved me. Didn't she? I thought she did. I loved her. Wait a minute...

"You're a cat."

You think? And your point is?

"Cat's don't talk. That's my point."

Says who?

"Everybody knows cats don't talk."

I know no such thing, stupid. Can you hear me?

"Well...yes."

Then I am talking! Stupid human, I'm so tired of you.

She yawned and put her head down, as if to say she was done tolerating my human stupidity.

"I don't understand."

Of course you don't. You're human, and you're stupid.

"Can you please stop calling me stupid? You're giving me a complex."

Oh poor baby, a human with no self-worth, drenched in self-doubt, and self-pity...stupid whore.

I asked her not to call me stupid, and she tags whore onto it?

"Why am I a whore?"

Trying to sell yourself, aren't you?

"What? No...it's not like that."

You don't sound so sure.

"I'm not selling my body for sex. I'm selling a book."

You are selling thoughts from your mind, aren't you?

"Well, yes, I guess so, but it's a story."

It's a part of you for sale. That makes you a whore.

"It's not the same thing!"

There was no reply. Her eyes were closed, and she seemed to be napping. Apparently she couldn't stay awake long enough to finish the conversation.

"Stupid cat," I muttered.

I heard that, whore, and I'm not the one who's stupid.

I shook my head in an attempt to shake loose the thought of her voice. I was simply overtired and frustrated. That was all, nothing more. Pity my imagination couldn't serve me as well when writing

"You have a nice nap there, Miss Bitchy."

She didn't respond. She didn't even bother to lift her head.

I returned to my laptop and placed my fingers on the keyboard, but I couldn't write. The sound of her voice rang in my head. It sounded eerily familiar, and that accent…it was bizarre to say the least. Delusional and in need of a chemical cocktail was looking more like my future than my fear.

"Enough," I said aloud, "Get back to work."

Work — you mean your pathetic attempt to write something someone would actually read, let alone publish? Don't make me laugh.

I spun my chair around and saw her looking at me again. She seemed annoyed.

"You mean cackle, right? Because you cackle, you don't laugh."

I laugh. Just because you don't find it honey to your ears does not make it any less a laugh. And who is Miss Bitchy? That is not my name. Call me by my name. After all, you named me, yet you forget it, and you wonder why I call you stupid.

"I didn't forget your name, I was being sarcastic."

Is Miss Bitchy one of your friends? Oh sorry, you don't have any of those…occupational hazard.

"Occupational hazard — I don't understand?"

Of course you don't, stupid whore. You understand nothing. You have no friends being the failure of a writer that you are. Who would want to keep company with you?

"You would, apparently."

She threw me a menacing glare.

You chose my company, I did not choose yours. You, I am stuck with, stupid, thankless whore.

I was growing weary of her name calling. Not only was I a stupid whore (according to my cat, or the demon in denial that resided within her), but I was a thankless one at that.

"Maybe you should just go back to your napping, Virginia, and let me get back to my work."

Stupid whore remembered my name, did she? Your work, ha! Don't make me laugh.

And with that, she pretended to be napping again. Or maybe she really was this time. If this kept up, she'd be taking a dirt nap. I smirked at the thought, feeling rather superior, until anxiety crept in.

What if I still heard her voice after she was dead? Did I really believe it was her voice? Was I actually thinking of putting her down to silence her? Was my cat possessed by a demon—one who liked to use the words *stupid* and *whore*?

I looked at Virginia. She continued napping. Part of me wanted to pick her up, place her on my lap, and stroke her beautiful grey fur. Another part of me wanted to strangle every last word out of her furry throat.

What was I thinking? I loved my cat. I could never harm her, but that voice, was I making it up? Was it part of a story? It had to be. It was the fatigue, frustration, and stress from writing. That was all, nothing more.

***

I woke, my head on my laptop, drool dribbling down the side of my face and in between the keys on the keyboard. I heard a woman's voice. At least I thought I did.

"Wake up, for Christ's sake," said Allie.

"You're back from the visit with your parents?" I asked my roommate.

"No, that was last month. I was with Damon, my boyfriend. Don't you remember?"

"Sorry, Allie, I've been working a lot."

"I can see that," Allie said and leaned over me, looking at the screen of my laptop.

"What's the word count on this? It looks like you finished your novel," she said as she scrolled through the pages I had apparently typed.

"I don't know, I haven't checked. I didn't even know I wrote all that," I responded.

"How long has it been since you slept?" Allie asked. "And I mean in bed, not drooling all over your keyboard?"

"No idea," I said.

"Have you been eating?"

"I think so."

"You think so? Have you been taking your medication? Well, have you, Virginia?"

"Virginia — you can hear her too? Wait, where is she?"

Allie looked both confused and horrified.

"Where is who, Virginia?"

"Yes, Virginia, where is she?" I asked.

Allie stood gaping at me. I wasn't sure why. Maybe she'd forgotten we had a cat.

"Here kitty, kitty, kitty," I called.

"Who are you calling?" Allie asked.

"The cat, Virginia, of course," I responded. "Wow, Al, maybe *you* need medication. I can't believe your forgot we have a cat."

"Virginia, we don't have a cat," Allie said.

"Virginia *is* the cat, Allie, what's wrong with you?"

"You think you're a cat?" Allie asked looking quite concerned.

"What? No, I'm not a cat, Virginia is."

Allie pulled up a chair and sat next to me, a grave look blanketed her face.

"I want you to listen to me carefully," she said.

"Alright, I'm listening."

"We do not, nor have we ever had a cat. Do you understand?"

I looked at Allie and wondered what kind of game she was playing. Her boyfriend enjoyed tricking people and playing with their heads. Maybe Allie had decided to play a trick on me. How could she not know about Virginia? I decided to play along and see where it went.

"Right, Allie, we don't have a cat."

That's right!" Allie said, as if I were a child who got a difficult math problem correct.

I smiled at her.

She dropped her chin to her chest and stared at me, the tips of her eyelashes touching her eye brows. She looked as if she were attempting to inspect my mind with her hazel eyed stare, searching for a sign that would assure her I was sane.

"You scared me there for a minute, Virginia. Where are your meds? I want to make sure you haven't missed any?"

"Virginia?" I replied and laughed. "Still playing are we, Al?"

The color in Allie's face drained taking with it the look of relief she had just moments prior.

"*You* are Virginia," she said sternly.

"I'm a cat?" I asked, playing along.

Allie got up abruptly and picked up the telephone. She began dialing as she walked to the other side of the room.

"Yes, I need to speak to Dr. Bordeaux, it's an emergency. My name is Allie Muller, and I'm calling for my roommate, Virginia Willington."

Allie stepped outside the room to continue her telephone conversation, but I could still hear her.

"She is Dr. Bordeaux's patient and she seems to..." her voice trailed off as she walked down the hall and into her bedroom.

I sat staring at my laptop screen. I began scrolling and looking at the pages I had typed. Why couldn't I remember writing any of it?

We get a lot done when that nosey ninny isn't here, don't we, stupid?

I turned around, and there sat Virginia. She looked at me with her glassy, green eyes. Her whiskers twitched as she smiled.

"Yes, apparently we do," I said.

This one might even get published, it's that good.

"You think so?"

I do, however; you won't be signing any publishing contracts in a straight jacket. The hands aren't exactly accessible in such, are they?

Her glassy, green eyes sparkled. She was right. If Allie managed to pull off her plot and get me locked up, I'd be indisposed for who knows how long.

"I bet that's the objective of the whole game she and Damon have going. Get me in the psycho ward and game over, she wins. The two of them would then have the entire apartment to themselves," I said.

Well, what are you waiting for, the men in the white coats to come and take you away? Get to it!

I looked at Virginia, and she at me, as she always did.

"What do you mean?"

You know what I mean...get rid of her! Quick, get in the kitchen before she comes back.

I jumped out of my chair and went into the kitchen. I stood near the stove and waited for Allie to return.

"Dr. Bordeaux is on vacation, so they're going to have another doctor call here, and I want you to—"

Allie stopped talking when I hit her on the back of the head with a frying pan. She stumbled and fell to her hands and knees.

That's not how your granddad taught you...do it right!

I glared at Virginia. I knew what she meant, and I hated it. My four sisters and I had to help my grandfather on the farm when we were kids. Since I was the oldest, I had to help him with the worst of the chores—the really messy ones.

Don't look at me like that! Do what needs to be done!

I got the carving knife out of the draw and walked over to Allie who was still on her hands and knees. I grabbed a handful of Allie's blonde hair, pulled her head back, and did what Granddad had taught me. He said it was humane. A clean kill is what he called it. I thought it was disgusting.

It's about time... what if she had started screaming? Instead of the men in the white coats, it would be the men in blue uniforms coming to take you away... stupid.

Allie made an odd sound before crumpling to the floor in a pool of sticky red yuck. There was no way she could scream...at least...not now.

She wasn't a bad roommate, as roommates go. She was always nice to me, but she invited her boyfriend Damon over a lot. I got tired of listening to them go at it. I swear she was loud on purpose, to annoy me, and to try to make me jealous.

I didn't have a boyfriend. I never had a boyfriend. Allie had had several since she moved in, sometimes two at a time, and all of them had money. Every one of them bought her expensive gifts. One of them even bought her a car.

I looked at Virginia, and then back at Allie.

"She slept around with men who had money. I think she did it to get stuff. See that gold watch she's wearing? One of them bought her that. One of them bought her that fancy sports car she drives too. She's a — "

Whore?

I shrugged my shoulders. "I guess."

I turned my eyes away from Allie, hers now frozen in a fixed stare, and looked again at Virginia.

"Maybe she was a whore...maybe she was just a slut."

Virginia let out a roaring laugh, her evil cackle louder than ever. Then she stopped abruptly and glared at me.

What are you waiting for? Clean up this mess! And make sure you use bleach. I don't want that whore's blood staining the kitchen tile.

Use the pages from your old manuscript to soak up the blood. What a waste of trees that crap you called a novel is. That paper isn't good for much now, besides...

Virginia's voice faded as I mopped Allie's blood with the pages of my old manuscript and put them into a trash bag. Allie had a lot of blood in her for a small woman. I didn't think my old manuscript was going to be enough to do the job.

I looked in the cupboard under the kitchen sink and found a package of white paper towels. I opened them, ripped several off the roll, and watched them become red as they made contact with the bloody mess Allie had made.

Virginia rambled on.

Of course, the manuscript that is on your laptop...that will be a best seller, because I helped you write it. You're too stupid to write without me... when are you going to realize that? And now you won't have to suffer the shame of being a whore. Oh look... you missed a spot... no, stupid ... over there!

I looked up. Virginia had a paw extended pointing to an area I had over looked. I hurried to clean the spot, as Virginia blathered on about the novel, her brains, and my lack of brains, referring to me as stupid again.

I wasn't sure why Virginia thought as long as she helped write the book, I wasn't a whore. I didn't understand all of Virginia's reasoning I admit, but who can truly understand the reasoning of a cat?

Life Bleeds

Sybil cast aside the dead roses after removing them from the vase that had held them. She proceeded to empty the stagnate water, but it was not water that poured out, it was blood. Thick, bright, and red was the fluid that splattered onto to the stark, white porcelain of the kitchen sink.

It would leave a stain, most certainly. Not unlike the stain life had left on her soul from the pain, from all the bloody suffering. The stains of life were memory markers, each leaving a scar of remembrance, refusing to be forgotten.

Life bleeds in so many ways, she thought.

Just a Taste

There wasn't much to be thought about, nothing much to speak of, yet I'd think it anyway. The wee hours would escape me as if in a trance as my mind wandered.

The silence was shattered by the howling of wolves. Pack animals, both nocturnal and noisy—about what, I can only speculate.

Had they, in their numbers, stalked a prey, pounced, and ended the life of a weaker animal in a bloodthirsty killing? Perhaps.

Was it the waxing moon, gaining in her power, in her size, that stirred something within their beastly hearts? Possibly.

Were they just out and about, being obnoxiously loud at an hour when most humans slept? Apparently.

But whatever the reason for their howling it woke my husband who turned to my side of the bed.

"What the hell was that?" he whispered.

"Well", I responded, "it was certainly not I, for here I am in our bed. I am not out in the middle of the night on a bloodthirsty quest, howling at the moon, being obnoxiously loud at an hour while you're sleeping."

He looked at me a bit confused, but nevertheless began a sermon about the safety of walking about at night. The howling of those beasts, he reasoned, made his case.

Why would he feel the need to give such a sermon, you ask? Let's just say I've been known to wander about late at night into the wee hours of the morn, something that unsettles him in his concern for my safety.

I let him have his say and then I had mine.

"They wouldn't bother me, not one of their own."

(My husband likes to tease that I'm part wolf because I can smell things more acutely than other people and sense things animals do. I often communicate with the family dog without spoken commands and like to use my teeth for more than eating.)

My husband was not amused with my musings and told me so. He scolded me yet again, explaining once more how it was not safe to wander about in the dark, late at night, when we lived so close to the woods.

"Just listen to those howling animals, dangerous they are," he concluded. "Did you hear me?"

He wanted to know!

"I heard you," I answered.

I smiled at him, leaned over, and bit the bare flesh on his shoulder.

"Ouch," he said as he winced. He then requested I not draw blood.

I explained I had no intention of drawing blood, and I kissed the flesh I had just bitten.

He looked at me, his steel-blue eyes blazing with question.

"I just wanted to bite you," I said, answering the obvious question in his eyes.

He offered a smile that conveyed several things, rolled over, and went back to sleep.

They don't bother their own kind. I'll wander if I wish, and I'll bite when I please. I'll think even when there isn't much to be thought.

A mind is a peculiar thing to taste.

Sweet Death: Savor the Aroma

11 January, 1996

Dear Morbid Candle Company,

I am writing to let you know how much I enjoy your newest candle fragrance, Sweet Death. You see, I was throwing a holiday party for some close friends, and I wanted everything to be dead perfect. I purchased thirteen of your Sweet Death fragranced jar candles. I placed them all over the house and lit them. How utterly noxious their scent! The entire house smelled of sweet death. My guests were amazed. They thought I had spent days placing rotting corpses about the house when in truth all I had done was light your candles!

I can't thank you enough. You made the preparation for my party so much easier. It would have taken me weeks to acquire enough bodies, and days to allow them to ripen, not to mention the time it would have taken to put them in closets, behind the sofa, and such. Thanks to you, all I had to do was light your candles to achieve the same deathly aroma and ambiance. I will be sure to tell all my friends, and I will certainly buy more of your candles in the future, especially when entertaining.

Yours in death always,
Mrs. Dementia Mortem

P.S. I heard a rumor that next year you are coming out with another new fragrance called Warm Blood. I hope it's more than just a rumor. I have vampire friends who will go wild for it!

Warm Blood: The Imitation Red Lady

23 July, 1998

Dear Morbid Candle Company,

I am writing to offer my thanks in regard to your decision to pull your latest candle fragrance, Warm Blood, from store shelves. The experience I had whilst this candle fragrance was being burned was beyond the pale. From the news reports, I understand such happenings are not confined to the remote area in which I live.

You see, I attended a neighbor's party. They are vampires, and while I do consider them friends, I do not usually attend their parties as they partake of the Red Lady, and I do not. (I'm not judging, of course, it's their choice how they live their undead lives, and I wouldn't want you to think me prejudice of their kind.) However, this time I thought I'd give it a go and attend their latest bash. Lady Vildabloth had personally invited me to thank me for recommending your newest candle fragrance, Warm Blood, which she told me she would be burning at her party.

Well, she had lit no less than thirty-three Warm Blood candles in her large Victorian home. The place utterly reeked of blood. Sir Vildabloth had been detained by the police whilst transporting humans to his home. He was lucky not to be arrested for possession! Clearly those poor souls were mules for the Red Lady. Once he finally arrived, the vampire guests nearly overdosed because their thirst was so fierce due to the scent of your candles!

From there, things went from bad to worse. Werewolves began showing up due to the strong blood scent of your candles. They were salivating everywhere looking for fresh meat. It was repugnant to see these beasts prowling about Sir and Lady Vildaboth's property looking for something to tear to shreds. From what I understand, the family cat was consumed in a most distasteful manner, leaving the Vildaboth children heartbroken that their beloved pet Plasma was gone.

Please do not second guess your decision to pull this fragrance from store shelves. I sincerely hope you will be discontinuing it all together.

Yours in death,
Mrs. Dementia Mortem

Fresh Kill:
Biting Off More than You Can Chew

30 October, 1999

Dear Morbid Candle Company,

I am writing to complain about your newest candle fragrance, Fresh Kill. After the disastrous results from your last fragrance, Warm Blood, I thought your company would have learned a lesson with blood fragrant candles, and ceased production of them all together.

We have had numerous problems with werewolves prowling the streets and killing family pets when the vampires burn this fragrance because Warm Blood is no longer available. My neighbor Lady Vildaboth, who is a vampire, tells me that the vampire family down the street finds this scent to be so close to Warm Blood that they can't resist burning it daily.

We have had to telephone animal control on several occasions because of the problem your candle fragrance has caused. Unfortunately, the werewolves have killed and consumed several of the animal control officers, and they will no longer respond to our complaints. Werewolves usually go for less conspicuous prey such as cats, dogs, raccoons, and the like, but I suppose they took offense when the animal control officer tried to put that dog-catcher looped leash, or whatever it's call, around their necks!

I must ask you to please consider pulling Fresh Kill from store shelves immediately! I have asked my vampire friends, the Vildaboths, to write you as well as they have lost yet another family pet to werewolves.

While I remain a great fan of your candle fragrance Sweet Death, I will not be purchasing it anymore.

Until such a time when all your blood scented candles are pulled from store shelves, production of them discontinued, and no future blood scented candles released, I cannot in good conscience continue to support your company with my purchases. This saddens me greatly as I have heard that next year you are planning to release a scent called Funeral Fresh which I was so excited to try. Not only will I be giving up the aroma of Sweet Death, but I will never know the scent of a home that is Funeral Fresh.

Signed,
Mrs. Dementia Mortem

Brewing Life

In my cauldron is a potion for you,
I brewed to bring life from the grave;
I know it is a forbidden thing to do,
But when have you known me to behave?

I know you prefer them fresh and ripe,
For the breathing are best to reap;
So I poured it down the old drain pipe,
As I just did not think it would keep.

When the weather is warm and oh so fair,
You will find your fill easy this I know;
Many vibrant souls are but every where,
However once winter sets in it will slow.

I recorded the ingredients of the brew
Should you wish me to make it once more;
While it's far from ideal you could make due
If finding live ones becomes a chore.

Crazy Lady Stew

A house on Mourning Dove lane,
Lived a woman they called insane,
And every night she'd tell her tale
Whilst drinking dark and potent ale.

And as she'd drink her spirits down,
She'd speak of bones beneath the ground;
Of all the bodies she once held near,
And how she'd caused a town to fear.

She picked 'em clean and used 'em well,
For the butcher had no meat to sell;
She made a hearty and gruesome stew,
She made it secret and no one knew.

She fed the hungry and the poor,
She fed the homeless cats and more;
And when her secret was found out,
They deemed her insane without a doubt.

When they found remains of the dead,
She'd be put away for good they said;
But away she did not go, not quite,
For I sit and drink with her every night.

Beyond the Veil

The truth had long been concealed,
Whispered a voice beyond the veil;
In a grave manner she revealed,
What had caused her heart to fail.

She whispered of her sorrow,
She'd been forced to confess a lie;
Time no longer could she borrow,
She had been condemned to die.

Barefoot to the gallows she went,
The noose around her neck tight;
Soon her life would be spent
And her soul would take flight.

The floor gave way with a bang,
The weight of her body fell;
The witch, they said, must hang
And burn forever in hell.

The mob had been victorious,
She hanged for what they feared;
Her demise to them was glorious,
Each soul in attendance cheered.

Her body was buried deep,
Left to a worm-riddled decay;
Peacefully the town would sleep,
For a witch was killed that day.

The sun rose to a great plague,
Each person in town fell ill;
The cure appeared quite vague,
Few knew the healing skill.

For the healer they would wait,
One had passed the night before;
The townsfolk sealed their fate,
For the witch could heal no more.

The future contagious and bleak,
Death certain for each single one;
Beyond the veil they would seek
Forgiveness for what they had done.

Mortal Memory

Blood drips from my lip,
A thirst I cannot deny;
Unable to resist just a sip,
The veil of death draws nigh.

Come over here,
Closer, my dear,
I want to feel your pain;

Come nearer to me,
And you shall see
Mortality is life in vain.

Flesh trembles in my embrace,
Surrendering as death sets in;
A betrayed heart fails its pace,
As pallor blankets the skin.

Let go of your fear,
Release it, my dear,
Soon it shall no longer be;

On the threshold of peace,
Your pain will soon cease,
Of mortal memory you'll be free.

Haunted

The night bitter and damp,
The house chilly and dark;
The oil to light the lamp,
The walls, dingy and stark.

With you I talk and sit,
Your voice soft yet grim;
Your somber face moonlit,
A choice made on a whim.

My wounded heart now bleeds,
Your memory my burden to bear;
Regret on my tired soul feeds,
Your hanging birthed my despair.

Our bed empty and cold,
I no longer wish to be;
My future has been foretold,
At the gate, wait for me.

Squandered

Faded flower
Once so vibrant,
Wilted and withered
In water now stagnant
And reeking of rot.

Smooth as porcelain
And velvety soft,
Dreams that reached for the stars
From a bed in a loft
With wrinkled sheets.

Poetry sung
In a raspy voice,
Desperately wanting
A well planned choice
Never made.

A Fortnight

I came to you in darkness,
Aching and bitter cold;
In a fortnight, you said,
Everything shall be told.

I don't remember the days,
Or the nights for that matter;
Regrets and tears, so many,
In the wind memories scatter.

In a fortnight, you said,
The moon again shall wane;
The memories now are lost,
A life was lived in vain.

Leaving London

Lovely lady
Weaving words,
Tea and toast
For breakfast.

Broken heart,
Dispirited soul;
Jot a note
For the neighbor.

Wet towels,
Tape sealed doors;
No hope
Lit the oven.

Began in Boston,
Leaving London,
Rest peacefully
Lovely lady.

Rainy Day Mood

Pelting rain with many missions,
Scratch my pen, blood red ink;
Writing, bleeding, lettered admissions,
Swirl my spirit, down the sink.

Go on, you rainy day mood,
Endless aching of my bitter shame;
Through the hours, write and brood,
Go on and rain, rain, rain.

Sop my mind with a relentless storm,
Work my pen, the open door;
Weaving, rhyming, take your form,
Slip my feet, beneath the floor.

Go on, you rainy day mood,
Endless aching of my bitter shame;
Through the hours, write and brood,
Go on and rain, rain, rain.

Darkness in an Orange Sky

Light fades as it often does,
An orange sky sinks into the horizon.
A sickle moon remains,
The only light
In what now is
The darkness.

Leafless trees sway and dance
In a balmy breeze,
Evoking balmy thoughts;
Rattling my mind
Towards darkness.

Listen, they call
My name,
Into the darkness;
Whispering, the trees
My name,
The orange sky faded
Into darkness.

The Dark Garden

Dark and bitter cold,
Black and red blooms;
Such unforgiving soil,
A garden of tombs.

Time takes them,
Blossoms to weeds;
Empty hands,
Wind swept seeds.

Deep in the heart,
Saved for the morrow;
Melancholy grows,
A garden of sorrow.

Walking Wounded

Diseased
Yet disinfected,
The presence of death
Unseen to the naked eye.

Smile and nod
Bleed and wretch;
You've nothing left
They want.

Invisible wounds
To be seen;
Closed eyes
See nothing.

Marion

Whisper white and empty,
A blank page,
A still pen;

Aching pain and plenty,
A string of words,
A lion's den.

Write well and perhaps,
A good read,
A time when;

Fall back and relapse,
An empty basket,
A barren hen.

Fall

Flowers in a garden
Of memories laced with heartache,

Withering in the cold
As autumn creeps in.

A sun that sets too soon
Leaving darkness to find me.

The seasons keep changing.
And I'm never the same.

Echo of Time

Time passes as it remains still,
I'm shown an emptiness nothing can fill;
I'm reminded how much I have to lose,
The path we walk, we alone choose.

Death waits in silence stalking its prey,
By the shadow of night and the light of day;
Capturing and consuming every last soul,
Each one destined, devoid of control.

Hunted by a memory that insists,
I return to the past as it persists;
Haunted by a life that is no longer mine,
Lost am I in the echo of time.

Stitch

Lost in thoughts
Found after forgetting;
I wish
I would never remember.

Drowning in feelings
Felt after knowing;
I want
My mind washed clean.

Sick in spirit,
An aching soul;
I wish
I could erase time.

A sleeping vengeance
Will soon wake;
I want
My heart sewn shut.

Within Without

Cannot hide,
Face of death;
Fearful mask,
Stolen breath.

Mounting panic,
Beating heart;
Theater mask,
Mournful part.

Slipped away,
Bleeding ache;
Fallen mask,
Haunting wake.

Bleed My Dear

It was in a whirling madness, dear,
Truth shown through quite crystal clear;
My voice befell your lonesome ear,
Though you pretended not to hear.

Close your eyes and just let go,
Even if you wish not to know;
Rest assured the memories I shall save
For a time and place beyond the grave.

You asked this of me. You wanted me near.
I've grow impatient with your fear.
Gather the emotions that evoke a tear,
Pick up your pen and bleed, my dear!

Let me out! You've held me in!
You've drowned me in your imaginary sin.
You've silenced my words and my voice;
You took from me what was your choice.

Bleed my dear, now open a vein,
You mustn't fear you'll fall insane;
You mustn't try and silence me,
For this is how we set you free!

A Dark Quill

With a dark quill
Fashion a fate,
Perhaps suffering
That shan't abate.

Perhaps the falling
Of many a tear,
Perhaps the horror
Of many a fear.

Perhaps the sorrow
Of one's last breath;
Grief that consumes,
A loved one's death.

Dark quill and ink,
Crafts many a tale;
Imagination runs free,
Vengeance sets sail.

Scapegoat

Hang the blame on me,
The one you cannot own;
I am the scapegoat,
Cast at me your stone.

My shoulders are wide,
Upon them you place;
Your version of truth,
Reality you cannot face.

It circles back around,
It shall render its due;
Ignorance is the cover,
The day you shall rue.

The mirror of veracity,
You hide from its glare;
Hang your shame on me,
The one you cannot bear.

Row

The pain has worn me raw and thin,
Take a breath and we'll begin;

The radiating ache deep within,
There's a sinister measure to your grin.

The shine of the metal it grazes my skin,
The burden of memories laced with sin;

The countless times I let you in,
Bear my weight and take it on the chin.

Red Lace Poison

Her heart so bitter,
Envious hunger,
Ravenous and parasitic;
Maggots she flocks.

Red lace poison,
Whispering to her
Spiteful, distorted mind;
Froth she squawks.

Seething compost heap
Continually fed
Vengeful thoughts
In mists of red.

Red lace poison,
Prideful concern,
Slave to a queen;
Royalty she stalks.

Adoring reflection,
Penning her likeness,
Gazing upon a foul pout;
Mirrors she gawks.

Delusions festering,
Viciousness inbred;
Her vile ink and paper,
Drew my likeness dead.

Grave Dust Woman

You belong among the led,
Vain and vindictive —
Envy is bred.

You belong among the bled,
Shameless and sadistic —
Soil saturated red.

You belong among the dead,
Decayed and distorted —
Worm infested head.

Dish Rag

Hanging
Tattered
Worn and used;

Dingy
Forgotten
Labeled and bruised.

Thrown
Discarded
Wet and thin;

Judged
Scorned
Guilt and sin.

Mended
Washed
Hung and dried;

Understood
Excused
Mindful and eyed.

Whispered Lies

Can't be trusted,
Broken and rusted,
Bury the thoughts of doubt.

Through a clenched jaw grin,
Shouldn't have let you in,
Now there's now way out.

Sweet lies were whispered,
Grew and festered,
Used me for what I was worth.

Now that it's done,
With a new one you've begun,
More lies in need of birth.

The Indoctrination

We have good news
To share with you;
No need to question
What you should do.

Don't think for yourself,
You'll get confused or lost;
We've got all your answers,
And they've all been glossed.

Only we speak the truth,
And there is much to fear;
Yet with us you'll have hope,
To our rules you must adhere.

This way to the promise,
Our unquestioning sheep;
But should you speak out,
Guilt upon you we'll heap.

For we know too well,
If the facts you should see;
We will lose our control,
And away you shall flee.

We condemn all the others,
Evil transforms into light;
While we keep you distracted,
We're the evil in plain sight.

Nihility

An endless glowing,
A want-less knowing,
An emptiness all my own;

There's nothing to say,
Time persists each day,
Your colors you have shown.

Did you think I'd forget?
Perhaps filled with regret
For what you came to be?

Of nothing I was sure,
But this that had no cure,
Cut my soul to set it free.

She Was Here

I bit my tongue
Each distortion told;
Swallowing truth,
Swimming—
Rivers of doubt.

I held my breath
Purple and blue;
Each word that cut,
Bruised within
And without.

Always pulling,
Knife sharp picking
At the seams—
Dots of blood,
Tore it apart.

I saved the pins
You pricked me with;
Melted them down,
Fashioned a blade,
Plunged it into your heart.

Here nor There

Time empty,
Bitter cold;
My soul taken,
My sanity sold.

Always brave
But hardly bold;
Thoughts bought,
Secrets told.

Here nor there
And round about;
Cut me open,
Bleed me out.

Little within
But more without;
Lingering memory,
Eternal doubt.

Consumed

Raven eyed demons
In the still
Of the night;

Raven winged demons
Eat my soul
And take flight.

Little bird singing
In the tree
On the hill;

Little liar singing
Eat my heart
Get your fill.

Proof of Life

Pain within,
Pain without,
Death dances
And circles about.

Reflective blade
Across my skin,
Mirrored metal
Bleed my sin.

Smarting demon
Release the pain,
Proof of life
Down the drain.

Subconscious Fiction

Time burns when you're not here,
The day's endless, the night's cold;
My heart tattered, torn and seared,
My memory burdened with secrets you told.

I needed you in ways I never knew,
Your love filled me to the brim;
Aching silence laced in morning dew,
My day's dark, my night's grim.

I see your face when I close my eyes,
I hear the tone of your voice;
Words you spoke, honey laced lies,
Believing you was always my choice.

You visit me often in dreams,
You lie so beautifully with that smile;
A subconscious fiction not as it seems,
Bloodied and broken, you dance all the while.

To The Lighthouse

To the lighthouse we must go
It's time to say good-bye;
A beacon of light in the dark,
Darling, please don't ask me why.

I'll bring the bricks and rope,
You bring the paper and ink;
We'll pen a note of farewell
And together we shall sink.

Death is not the end,
The ocean brings a new tide;
But living without you, my dear,
Is an agony I cannot abide.

So to the lighthouse it is,
And to the sea, deep and cold;
Bound and weighted together,
We shall never grow old.

The Weight of Us

Eternal ache
In a forgotten soul,
Eternity penned
On a fragile scroll;
The scales
Have much to weigh.

Perpetual existence
In a forgotten way,
Fate fallen
On a stony brae;
Emptiness increases
The weight of us.

No Good Deed

My breath, a death
The beating of my heart;
My will, a kill
You're tearing me apart.

My life, a knife
Everything is withering;
My pain, a vein
The darkness is slithering.

Breathe the sorrow free,
Let it slip away;
Bleed it out of me,
Scrape loose the decay.

Your death, my breath
Pale grey ashes scattered.
Your will, my chill
Precious memories tattered.

Your life, my strife
Time is truth's lost daughter.
Your pain, my vein
Blood is diluted by water.

Open wounds seasoned with salt,
There is no good deed;
History locked in death's vault,
Roots the strangling seed.

Bottles and Bones

Deep in the earth,
Decayed vessel —
A life lived
Now perished.

Dirt covered remains,
Existence erased —
You've succumbed
And it's over.

Nothing but memories,
Old photographs —
All that's left
Are bottles and bones.

A Length of Rope

At the bottom of a bottle
Solace cannot not be found;
It's empty and it's bitter,
It's circling back around.

He's barely hanging on,
Trying to keep his head;
All the bottles are empty,
And he's filled with dread.

They whisper to him,
They understand his woe;
They promise to wait,
For soon he shall go.

A good length of rope,
And a rickety old stool;
Numerous are the ways
Life can be cruel.

Cemetery Trees

In a row
They stand,
Witnessing
The birth
Of death.

Tombs flank
Their trunks,
Offering
All those
Lacking breath;

A place
To rest
Eternally,
Their bodies
To decay.

In the wind,
Their leaves
Whispering,
Of spirits
Passed away.

Surrounded By the Dead

I'm surrounded by the dead,
Their memories in my head,
Their photographs by my bed,
I ponder what lies ahead.

Their thoughts through me seep,
Their pains ache and weep,
Their agonies cut quite deep,
My words through them seep.

My writings are their choice,
The whispers are their voice,
In remembrance they rejoice,
Their memories are my choice.

I must pen all they have said,
To the passage I'll be lead,
I am often filled with dread,
I'm surrounded by the dead.

The Living Dead

We're dead,
They don't know,
Nor do they care;

They think
We will answer,
And always be there.

We gave
All we could,
They took every bit;

We faded,
They don't see
'Twas life we quit.

Rotting away,
As we are,
It'll come to be;

One day
They shall know,
Death set us free.

Through the Veil

I am drifting,
Images slithering,
Passed are the souls I see.

Voices are whispering,
Memories are filtering,
They are coming for me.

Death is eternity,
Peaceful certainty,
Nothing left to say;

Letting it release,
Consciousness cease,
I have passed away.

Grave Spirits

Grave state of spirits,
Filtering—
Ever fiber of being,
Tainting its touch,
Takes too much.

Quiet numbing,
Took shape,
Began feeding;
Parasitic sin
Buried within.

Grave conditioned spirits,
Whispering—
Bones of the past,
Worn out soul,
Swallowed whole.

Sullen and sickened,
Disease ridden state;
A veinal poison slithering,
Spirits keep withering.

Ignis Fatuus

Maybe none of it was real,
In illusion again I'm caught;
Created from imagination,
Dredged the depth of thought.

Melancholy spectacles found me,
Dark glass with colorless view;
Maybe none of it was real,
Slept the part of me that knew.

Awoke to a harsh reality,
Skin of the facade I must peel;
Once again questioning reality,
Maybe none of it was real.

Passage

The closed door
Is locked no more
Slip past the illusion of pain.

The last place
A lingering embrace
Death comes to take us again.

The passage in death,
Exhale your last breath
Release me my love so dear;

Rest till we again wake,
Remembrance I shan't forsake,
Eternity shall soon be here.

The Little Death

Awake and remember the pain,
Forget, forget—just fall insane.
Madness lingers in absence of light,
The worse it gets, the more you fight.

Darkness persists and consumes the day,
Forget, forget—sleep it away.
Melancholy whispers in a haunting breath,
Slumber sweetly, the little death.

When Mountains Crumble

I am haunted,
The memories
Whisper
Penetrating
My mind;

I am wanted,
Dreams implore,
Insist
Demanding
I recall.

I am taunted,
The pain
Radiates
Whirling
I find;

I am daunted,
Mountains crumble,
Defeated
Broken
So small.

Commanding Calm

Hemorrhaging emotions everywhere,
Bite your tongue and walk away;
Nothing is free, nothing is fair,
Another piece of you dies today.

The ravenous rage rotting inside,
Take a deep breath, nod and smile;
Nothing to say but lots to hide,
It won't seem so bad in a while.

Stiff upper lip shed no tears,
Strength is something you earn;
Slip past your worthless fears,
Learn to sit and take the burn.

Released emotions transform,
Stop faltering the time is now;
Find the calm within the storm,
Dead center from stern to bow.

Indifference

The memories,
Laced with pain;
What remains is
Woven with
Regret.

Images flash,
Thoughts linger;
Memories fill every
Corner
Yet it remains
Empty.

Time filters,
Years skip;
A desolate garden
Blooms
Every shade of
Heartache.

The future,
Shadowed in despair;
Your light
Once so bright,
Faded into
Indifference.

Perhaps

I'm not giving up,
You're not giving in;
Labeled and worthless,
Silk spun imaginary sin.

I've nowhere left to hide,
You've nowhere to go;
Gaping wounds taunt us,
A needle and thread to sew.

Time is catching up now,
We can never run that fast;
We're fading into memory.
Soon we'll be the past.

A Measure of Time

Time is a persistent illusion,
Minutes and hours each a delusion;
Days and weeks, merely confusion,
Years bleeding, perpetual contusion.

Time is an invented state,
Minutes and hours are never late;
Days and weeks, refusing to abate,
Years weaving, hallucinations create.

Time is a liar and a thief,
Minutes and hours require belief;
Days and weeks, little relief,
Years burning, habitual grief.

Time is an end to a means,
Minutes and hours reality seems;
Days and weeks, perhaps dreams,
Years breeding, time streams.

Aim

I wished it here
And I watch it fly,
From the northern corner
Of the eastern sky.

The weary traveler
I had come to be,
Many lonely miles
Now far behind me.

I had touched the sky,
A glistening golden hue;
My soul was reminded
Of all it once knew.

Yet in time it faded
And it flew once more,
From the southern corner
Of the western shore.

The Poets

Time stole an art once known.
Frozen in centuries is an hour.
Quill and paper fell dead to time.
Have the words lost their power?

The meter and melody of music,
Whisper such beauty once said;
Tears of a bittersweet symphony,
Perhaps all the poets are dead.

Thoughts but seeds of words,
Plant and bloom they may;
Ink and paper keep willing,
The words will have a way.

Beautifully Grim

The beauty of the poetic,
The reality of the grim;
Create a lovely poison,
Consume it on a whim.

The stillness of silence,
Dark rivers run too deep;
Create a plausible reality,
Your sanity you can keep.

Life is a series of moments,
Caught in fragments of time;
Gather them while you can,
The clock soon shall chime.

Blood thread woven tapestry,
Emotion and memory entwined;
The joyful and the beautifully grim,
Perhaps it is all a state of mind.